"Why do you really hate men so much?"

Tamsin caught her breath at Blaise's question, shocked. Wordlessly she looked out the window seeing the image of Nigel's face as it had been once—and tears filled her eyes.

"Why?" he repeated and turned her around and saw her face before she could blot out the memories.

"Leave me alone," she said in a whisper.

"Someone hurt you." He said it, and it wasn't a question. And his tone wasn't mocking or sarcastic. His voice was almost gentle. Then he let her go and left without a word.

Tamsin had seen many expressions on Blaise Torran's face, but never before compassion. Now she had, and it was disturbing. She didn't want compassion from anybody, but particularly from him.

OTHER
Harlequin Romances
by MARY WIBBERLEY

The Taming of Tamsin

by

MARY WIBBERLEY

Harlequin Books

TORONTO • LONDON • NEW YORK • AMSTERDAM
SYDNEY • HAMBURG • PARIS

Original hardcover edition published in 1978
by Mills & Boon Limited

ISBN 0-373-02221-2

Harlequin edition published December 1978

PRINTED IN U.S.A.

CHAPTER ONE

'I'M sorry for the children, of course,' said Tamsin. 'But you know I don't like this kind of job. Can't someone else go?'

Her father looked up at her from his desk, and gave a wry smile. 'No,' he answered. 'You're ideal. It's only for four or five weeks, until the parents have sorted out their legal wrangles once and for all——'

'They never are sorted out properly,' cut in Tamsin bitterly. 'You've only got to read the papers to know that. "Tug of love" children, they call them—tug of hate more like, the way the parents carry on——'

'Then don't you think these kids deserve a break? They've been dragged all over the continent by their father until their mother managed to kidnap them, bring them back here and have them made wards of court. And now she's ill with it all, and terrified her ex-husband will trace them—which is why you're going to take them to this remote cottage which has no possible connection with their mother, and *look after them*. Okay?' He pushed a photograph across the desk at her. 'Take a look—go on, then say no.'

Tamsin picked up the photograph. Two cherubic faces beamed at her, a boy and girl of about six, the boy's arm protectively round his sister's shoulder, a teddy clutched firmly in his other hand.

'Oh,' she said. She looked at her father, and caught

the glint in his eyes before he managed to hide it. 'You crafty man,' she sighed, exasperated. 'You knew——'

'I knew once you'd seen the kids you wouldn't refuse.' He smiled complacently, and closed the buff folder, then handed it to her. 'You'd better read up all the details while I do some telephoning. It's going to be quite a cloak and dagger operation—and you leave at five tonight. Go in the blue Mini—it's old enough not to cause any attention. The address of the cottage is in there—you can check up the map in the outer office. Off you go, love.'

Tamsin slid gracefully off the desk and stood up. 'I'm not sure it's such a good thing, working for one's parent,' she said decisively.

'Rubbish,' her father snorted. 'Where else would you have got such good training for nothing? A black belt in judo, brown in karate—expert on small arms——'

'Yes, and I daren't ever ask for a raise, dare I?' She hugged him affectionately. ' 'Cos you're too *mean*!'

He slapped her bottom. 'An old fool, more like. When I retire this place will be yours. Why, you'll probably be the only woman in England to run your very own private detective agency.'

'Hmm! *You'll* retire when you reach a hundred—I'll be an old lady myself by then——'

'Out! Make me a coffee, woman, and quick about it. And tell Pam not to put any incoming calls through for at least half an hour.'

'Yes, sir.' Tamsin saluted smartly, picked up the folder, and went out, closing the door behind her. She heard her father pick up the telephone and begin to dial as the door clicked shut.

She grinned at Pam, her father's middle-aged secretary who sat busily typing at her desk. 'No calls for half an hour, Pam,' she said. 'I'm going to make coffee, then study this. Want one?'

'Please, love. No sugar—I'm dieting again.' Pam sighed and patted her hips. 'Is that the Zandradi children's file?'

'Yes.' Tamsin put it down on a chair. 'What a mess! Poor little mites.'

Pam's face softened. 'I know. I'm glad you'll be looking after them. You like kids, don't you?'

'Yes, I suppose I do,' answered Tamsin with surprise. 'I've never really thought about it before, but with five nieces and nephews of assorted ages—and I get on well with them all—I suppose I must.'

Pam sighed. 'It will be like a holiday for them. They're not seven yet, you know. There's less than a year between them. You'll be giving them lessons?'

'If Dad wants me to.' Tamsin filled the kettle at the sink in the corner, and put it on. 'I'll take plenty of games too. I can scrounge some from my sister-in-law before I leave tonight. Am I taking the children down to the cottage?'

'Why, no, didn't your father tell you? Mr Torran will be——'

Tamsin whirled round. 'What?'

'Oh dear.' Pam's face fell. 'Didn't he say——'

Tamsin walked slowly over to Pam's desk and put her hands down on it, facing the older woman, whose face now registered comic dismay.

'You'd better tell me exactly what dear old Dad has been cooking up—and I can see by your expression that it's something he conveniently "forgot" to tell me.'

Pam cleared her throat. 'Hum, well—ah!' This

with great relief as the telephone on her desk shrilled loudly. 'Excuse me, love. Douglas Agency, can I help you?' she said smoothly. Tamsin left her to it and went to make the coffee. She was seething inwardly. She had *known,* she had just known there was something else—but she hadn't known what it was. Now a suspicion was forming in her mind, and the sooner she got it sorted out, the better.

She put a beaker of coffee on the busily talking Pam's desk, and carried the second one in to her father. He was just putting the telephone on his desk down.

'Right,' said Tamsin. 'No beating about the bush. Why didn't you tell me about this Mr Torran——'

'Ah,' said her father. 'Yes, well. I was going to——' there was a distinctly guilty look to his normally placid face, and Tamsin banged the beaker down on his desk. 'Careful—temper!' he said in jolly tones that didn't fool Tamsin for one moment.

'Damn your desk!' she shot back, 'and don't "temper" me. What is it you haven't told me?'

'Well, nothing *really*—only that you can hardly be expected to look after the children alone——'

'It's what you asked me to do, isn't it?' she cut in. '*And* I agreed—and you know damn well I'm perfectly capable——'

'Of course you are,' he soothed. 'My dear, *I* know that. You'd be more than a match for any average man——'

'Cut out the flattery, father dear, and get to the point.'

'Well, it's just that Mrs Zandradi would feel better if there was a man looking after them too, and she is my client, and paying well—so I could hardly——'

'You can. Okay, let him look after them!'

'Be reasonable, Tam. You can't have a man taking care of two small children for five weeks.'

'It's been done before. Listen, Dad, he's staying there as well, isn't he? At the cottage, I mean—I can see by your face. Now you know how I feel about men in general——'

'I know you're an unreasonable, quick-tempered little hussy who likes her own way,' her father interrupted. 'And I know I should have spanked you more when you were a child——'

'Thanks!' sparked back Tamsin. 'But if you think I'm sharing a cottage with a *man*—good grief! I'm surprised at you even considering the idea. He could be a wolf——'

'And you can be sure I went into *that* angle, my dear. I've discovered that he regards women in the same light that you regard men. In other words—he's a woman-hater.'

'I'm not going!' she insisted.

'Oh yes, you are. I just finished phoning. He's on his way down from Stirling right now, and he's expecting to meet you at the cottage at seven. So you see, you have no choice.'

For a moment their eyes met in a silent clash, father and daughter, he calm, very much the stern parent, she rebellious, her temper precarious. Then Tamsin shook her head. 'All right,' she said softly, temper fading rapidly. She knew when she was beaten. 'You win. But——'

'Ah, ah, don't spoil it.' His face softened. 'You're my daughter all right. Do you think I'd like it if you were all meek and mild? No, love, I wouldn't change you in any way. But in this matter, I have no choice.

You'll look after those kids perfectly—and once I saw the photo, I couldn't turn the job down either. Give them a break. It's not for long. This Torran fellow will be doing a job too, remember. He might not like being a sort of nursemaid to two lively kids, but he's taken the task on.'

She nodded. 'Right. What kind of car will he be in?'

Her father picked up his memo pad. 'A—Ford Granada, beige, P registered, nothing fancy, you see.'

'Have you a description of him?'

'No. He'll have the kids, that's enough.'

'I suppose so. I'll go and do my homework on that map. Sorry I snapped, Dad.' She gave him a little grin. 'A job is a job. I'll do all you want me to.'

'That's my girl! Now, I'm going out to lunch in half an hour. Anything you need?'

'Yes. Some games suitable for six-year-olds—I'll phone Sue and ask her, will you collect them?'

'Will do. Nothing else?'

She pulled a face. 'Yes—a bottle of aspirin. I'm getting a headache thinking about *him!*' She ducked and made for the door as her father aimed a duster at her. 'All right, I'm going to have my coffee with Pam like a good girl.' She heard him chuckle as she closed the door behind her.

At five she was on her way up the motorway to Yorkshire. It was already growing dark, the autumn evening closing in rapidly as she drove expertly up the M1. The map was beside her, the address of the cottage in the glove compartment, and on the back seat, beside her two suitcases, a stack of boxed games, some books, a thick pad of drawing paper, and a boxful of crayons. She switched on the radio and began to hum to the music that flowed out. She had a job to do, and she was a professional, like her father. The two children would be looked after, cared for, and allowed to forget all the unpleasantness that had dogged their young lives for the past year or so. Of the man called Torran, she thought not at all.

She needed all her concentration after leaving the motorway. Country roads were the very devil in the dark, especially in a part of the country she didn't know, and when at last she saw the lights of the village she sighed with relief. This was it, Hacklett, and the cottage was three miles past, then turn left, up the lane with a sign saying—if she was lucky—Black Lane Ends.

The village was left behind, and all was dark. There was no traffic on the road. In the distance the black Yorkshire hills towered darkly, and only the occasional glimmer of light twinkled from a cottage. She saw the sign, turned left, and drove up a steep narrow track. This was remote enough all right, the perfect hide-away for anyone. The rain lashed down on her windows, and wind rocked the car as she struggled up the steep road.

The cottage should be on the right, two hundred yards from the road, hidden by trees, any time now. She saw the wide gateway, the white fence, and turned. Then up an even narrower rutted track, narrower and narrower—then she saw it looming darkly ahead. Nothing moved, nothing stirred. She was alone. She shivered as she switched off heater and engine, and the car settled into stillness. The wind and rain buffeted the car, and it was no use sitting here, she had to go in. She opened her bag, found the door key, took a deep breath and ran out, slamming the car door behind her.

A minute later she was standing in the dark hallway. The house was silent and waiting. It was just
past seven and soon the children would be here.
Tamsin found the light switch and pushed. Light
flooded the hallway and she let out her breath. For
one moment she had dreaded that the power would be
off. Now to light a fire—it was freezing! She found
the lounge to her left, went in, switched on the light.
A fire was laid, the room was clean and dusted, and a
note was on the table in the centre of the room. She
picked it up and read: 'Dear Madam, I have cleaned
and aired bedding as requested. If you need me, my
telephone number is Hacklett 231. Yours faithfully, E.
Armstrong (Mrs).' Tamsin put the note down and
smiled. Someone—probably her father—had done
their work properly. Mentally thanking the absent
Mrs E. Armstrong, she went and put a match to the
newspaper, watched it blaze and catch the wood, then
went to explore the cottage.

There were three bedrooms, a lounge, another sitting room, and a large old-fashioned kitchen. As well
as a bathroom upstairs, there was a toilet and washbasin in a tiny room under the stairs. The cottage was
old, with solid walls and small leaded-paned windows.
After she had drawn the curtains, the lounge assumed
an air of warmth and cheer. She went out and fetched
in her luggage.

The refrigerator in the kitchen was stacked with
food and five pints of milk, and fresh vegetables filled
a rack by the back door. There were two bolts on both
back and front doors, and all the windows were
secure. That was something. Tamsin checked automatically. Then she went to the telephone in the hall

to call her father and make her first report. When that was done she filled two hot water bottles and put them in the twin beds in the third bedroom. She then made herself a cup of coffee and sat down to wait the arrival of her two charges, and the unknown Mr Torran.

A thunderous knocking at the front door roused Tamsin, and she sat up guiltily, realising she must have been dozing. She had bolted the front door, and then fallen asleep. She ran into the hall, undid the bolt and opened the door wide.

She hadn't known what she had expected to see. Some middle-aged, soft-featured man perhaps. That vague impression was banished instantly at the sight of the towering giant who stood on the step, hard-eyed, lean, unsmiling. He frowned.

'This *is* Myrtle Cottage?' he asked, as if it couldn't possibly be.

'Yes. And you are——'

'Blaise Torran. Don't tell me *you're* Miss Douglas?'

Her hackles rose. His tone wasn't insulting—not quite. It just escaped that. It expressed strong disbelief, almost astonishment.

'I am. Where are the children?'

'Asleep in the back of the car. Are you alone?'

No, I've got the Dagenham Girl Pipers in the lounge—was the retort she neatly nipped in the bud. What did he expect? 'Yes, I am,' she replied calmly—which was an effort. She swallowed. It was a pity her father hadn't had a photograph of this creature as well as the children. At least she would have known what to expect. That is, if she'd been mad enough to come. 'Shall we bring them in?' she managed to add.

'No, I will. Get their beds ready.' He turned and

vanished into the darkness. He didn't wait to hear her reply, he just went. Tamsin ran upstairs and opened the first bed, moving the bottle down to the feet. The next moment she heard him walking up the stairs. He carried in a sleeping child, teddy clutched in arms, and laid the boy in the bed. 'Just take his shoes off,' he said, 'it won't hurt them to sleep in their clothes for one night,' and went out. Tamsin eased the little boy's shoes off and covered him up. He hadn't stirred. Then she heard the man again, and had the bed open waiting. The girl stirred slightly and dropped the doll she had been carrying. Tamsin replaced it and bent over the sleeping child.

'Ssh,' she said gently. 'Go to sleep.'

She waited a moment, but neither moved. Quietly she went towards the door, and he was waiting outside, silhouetted darkly, the landing light behind him. There was nothing ordinary about him—and he was furious, that much was obvious from his face.

'Right,' he said quietly. 'Downstairs. I want a word with you.' He turned and went down, leaving her to follow. For a moment she stood there and watched the broad-shouldered man descend. He knew how to give his orders—and Tamsin didn't like it. As far as she was concerned, *she* was in charge. I want a word with you, he had said. You're not the only one who wants a word, she thought. And no man bosses me around! She smiled to herself and began to go slowly down the stairs. He was in for a surprise.

CHAPTER TWO

HE stood in front of the blazing fire and looked at Tamsin as she walked across the room towards him. 'I expected a woman, not a girl,' he said, 'someone capable of looking after two children——'

'Hold it!' Tamsin cut in. She stopped in front of him. 'What do you mean—a girl? I'm twenty-two.'

'You look about sixteen.' He glanced up her slowly, from toes to top of head. It was clear he didn't believe her.

'And you look like a bad-tempered swine,' she retorted smartly, 'which you probably are. And bossy with it. Well, you don't boss me around! So let's get that straight before we start. I don't know who you are and I don't really care. I'm here to take care of those two children upstairs and I intend to do so. I'm perfectly capable of doing so alone, just for your information——'

'Come off it!' The corner of his mouth lifted in scorn. 'How well do you think you'd cope if their father came looking for them with a couple of his friends?'

'I may look young, but I happen to have a black belt in judo and a brown one in kara——'

'Big deal!' His eyes narrowed.

'Don't be so sarcastic,' she snapped. 'Those two children have been through a bad time——'

'You don't need to tell me,' he said swiftly. 'That's why I agreed to bring them and stay with them. But I can do without added encumbrances, like quick-tempered girls——'

'Quick-tempered? Huh! Coming from you, that's rich. You storm in like a bulldozer, giving your orders before you've even drawn breath, you insult me—and you have the nerve to call *me* quick-tempered. Compared to you, I'm positively docile!' she finished.

He laughed. Tamsin lashed out to wipe the laughter from his face, because she had had just about enough —and he caught her hand, held it, and said softly, all laughter gone:

'Watch it, little girl. Let's see how strong you are, judo expert.' It was his smile that did it. She would show him. She *would*!

She twisted, bent—and he should have gone flying. Only something went wrong. He didn't. But worse— something else happened instead. He moved swiftly, and the next moment she was held, helpless in a grip of steel.

'Snap,' he said quietly. 'Two black belts—and I'm about six stone heavier than you. Now get out of *that*.'

'All right.' She relaxed. 'You've proved your point —whatever it was. Let me go.'

He released her, and she faced him defiantly. She would not show weakness in front of him, not ever. She lifted her chin. 'So you're a big strong man,' she said. 'Bravo! But are *you* capable of dealing with *men*?' It was sarcastic, said in the heat of temper, and she managed to inject scorn into her voice—and she knew the answer, just by looking at him. She had never seen any man so tough-looking in her life, and her father employed some in the agency who were tough enough to tackle anything or anyone—but this one was different. Well over six feet tall, shoulders broad and muscular, clad in denim shirt and jeans, he exuded a kind of power and strength rarely seen. Black-haired, dark brown eyes, a face that was hard and aggressive, needing a shave—which gave him a piratical appearance—he looked as if he could take on anyone in the world, and win.

He looked at her. 'I won't even bother to answer that,' he said. 'I'm hungry. Where's the food?'

'In the kitchen,' she snapped.

'Right, let's go and see what there is. Can you cook?'

'Yes. Can you?' She was still furious.

'Well enough, when I have to. You're here. You cook for me, okay?'

'If you ask nicely, I might. If you're going to speak like that, you can get your own food. I'm here to look after the children, not you.'

He lifted an eyebrow. 'So you keep saying. But we might as well have a sensible division of labour, don't you think?'

'Meaning?'

'What do you think I mean? Presumably you're intelligent—don't act dumb, it'll get you nowhere with me. Okay, so we're both here for one purpose. Let's get it quite straight now, while the kids are asleep. They have to be kept safely out of sight for a few weeks, and they have to be fed and clothed and entertained. Right? With me so far?'

His tone was that infuriating mockery that kept her temper at simmering point. And arrogant too. She disliked him—she had from the first moment he'd erupted into her life with his 'don't tell me *you're* Miss

Douglas?' and she wasn't prepared to start liking him any more now. 'I'm with you,' she said. 'Unfortunately.'

He ignored that last word, or seemed to anyway. 'Then, for that reason, we're working together. So you'll do the cooking and tending to their immediate needs——'

'And what will you do?' she flashed back. 'Supervise? I'll bet you're good at that!'

'There's no need to be rude,' he said calmly. 'What's your first name?'

'What's that got to do with it?' she demanded.

'Plenty. You're an aggressive little spitfire——'

Aggressive! she thought. That's good, coming from you. But she didn't say it. She waited. 'And we clearly don't like each other,' he went on. 'But while they— the children—are about, we will behave perfectly normally and politely to one another, because they have had just about as much as they can take over these past months, and I for one am going to see that their time here, in hiding, is as pleasant as I can make it—and if you don't like it you know what you can do. So—what's your first name?'

'Tamsin.'

'Right. Mine's Blaise. Any questions?'

'Yes. What are *you* going to do—in the way of actual work, I mean?' she asked sweetly.

'Enough. You'll see. Now, are you going to get me some food or not?' His dark brown eyes held hers, and she couldn't look away. It was all there in them, the hardness, the ruthlessness she had already sensed, and if she refused he would probably go without another word and prepare something for himself. And it wouldn't make life any easier.

'I'll do something,' she said. 'I'm hungry myself. I was waiting until you arrived before I made anything—I thought the children would be hungry.'

'They ate an hour ago at a motorway restaurant. I knew they'd be asleep before they reached here, so I made sure they had a meal. But I wasn't hungry. Now I am.'

Perhaps, somewhere, he had a heart. She doubted it, personally, but at least he had concern for his two charges. It was something. Some of the brittle tension had gone. She looked at him, and saw the change in his expression. 'What would you like?' she asked. 'There are tins of meat, and eggs——'

'Anything. Omelette if it's easy. I don't care.' She saw, just for a brief instant, the fatigue on his face, and something prompted her to say: 'I'll make you a drink first, and you can have it while I'm preparing the food. Tea or coffee?'

'Coffee. Black, no sugar.'

She went out of the room. The water in the kettle was still warm, and she put it on to heat while she found eggs and cheese. She was about to pour his coffee out when he walked into the kitchen and sat down at the table. 'Have you checked doors and windows?' he asked her.

'Yes. Everything's secure.'

'Good.' He looked around him. 'This is a good place. It's remote, but not too much so. Have you looked around outside?'

'No. It was dark when I arrived.'

He nodded. 'First thing in the morning I'll scout around. We want to get the cars out of sight if possible.'

'Why? Nobody knows mine.'

'But someone might know mine,' he said softly. She felt a prickle of something akin to fear. It was the way he had said it. She looked sharply at him.

'We'll use yours for shopping,' he said. 'I'll put mine away.'

For the first time, Tamsin realised exactly what kind of task she had undertaken. It had all seemed so easy—too easy. Now, seeing him, she wasn't sure of anything any more. Yet she wouldn't let him see that. She began to beat the eggs, while he watched her. He watched her until she began to feel uneasy, and it made her fingers clumsy. Pouring the egg mixture into the pan, she could no longer keep silent.

'What is it?' she asked. 'Why are you looking at me?'

'I'm seeing what kind of woman you are. Oh, I know you've told me you're tough. I'm not too sure about that. You may be. Or you may be the type who'll fold up at the first sign of trouble——'

'You think there might be some?'

'Anything's possible. Why do you think I'm here?' And it came again, that frisson, the merest tingle up Tamsin's spine. She took a deep breath. But she didn't answer, because she saw him clearly for the first time. Blaise Torran was no ordinary man; he was someone special. More than that, he was afraid of nothing. She knew that with a deep, sure instinct older than time itself.

'I'm beginning to realise,' she said slowly. The omelette was done. She slid it on to a plate and handed it to him. Then she buttered the bread. 'Don't worry, I won't "fold", as you put it.' She looked at him as she said it. 'I don't like the sort of battles that go on in divorce courts, where the children are used as pawns—and I suspect you don't either. And I may only look sixteen—as you so tactfully put it—but I'm older, and I hope, wiser than I was then.' Her eyes were a very clear blue, and her gaze on him was calm and determined, and she saw an answering spark in his own, darker eyes. He nodded.

'All right. Perhaps we're beginning to understand one another. You make a good omelette. Are you equally skilful at the other culinary arts?'

'Yes.' He wasn't modest, she saw no reason why she should be. 'I'm very good at most things—the children will be well fed.'

'Which reminds me.' He reached into his shirt pocket and brought out a folded piece of paper which he handed to her. 'Their likes and dislikes. Make a list of all you need and I'll go and get food in the morning.'

She sat down and studied it while he ate. Then she looked up. 'That seems straightforward. I'll check later, when I've eaten.' He had changed the subject, which was a relief. Perhaps, as long as they kept on safe, neutral topics, like food, they might get on better. Perhaps ...

'While you're eating, I'll phone their mother.' He looked at his watch. 'Then bed. We're getting up early in the morning.'

'What do you call early?'

'About seven.'

She smiled. 'That's *early*?'

'It is for me. Don't tell me—you're up with the lark at five every morning, right?'

She smiled sweetly. 'You had me worried for a moment then. I really thought you were becoming quite civil.' She stood up and went over to the cooker.

'I see I was wrong. Are you always sarcastic?'

He laughed, pushed his empty plate away, then stood up, carrying it over to the large old-fashioned sink. Then he stood behind her, close, much too close, but she didn't move away, or flinch. 'I don't think,' he said softly, 'that life is going to be dull with you around.'

Tamsin looked around at him, eyes flashing. 'It's a pity,' she retorted, 'that I can't say the same. You're a typical, boring, aggressive male!'

'Am I?' he seemed almost amused. 'You may find out just how aggressive I can be if you stay around long enough. No doubt you've had your own way up till now—judging by the way you talk. Well, miss, it won't work with me.'

She turned fully round to face him. Her eyes sparkled, her cheeks were pink with temper. 'Listen,' she breathed, 'I've had enough of you—and you've only been here an hour. Why don't you run off and phone, and leave me to enjoy my food in peace?'

'I'll go when I choose, not when you dismiss me.' He was much taller than she, also much too close— and he knew it, knew it made her uncomfortable—but he didn't care. He put out his hand and tipped her chin slightly. 'Just remember that.'

'Take—take your hand off me!'

'Make me,' he said softly, oh, so very softly.

Tamsin stood very still and quiet for a moment. She was trying very hard to control her breathing. Then she moved. She knocked his hand away swiftly and swung away from him, all in the same instant.

'See?' she exclaimed. 'It was easy—oh!'

He had swung her round again and held both her arms, lightly just beneath the elbows, and she knew that grip. It was impossible to break. 'Now try,' he said.

'I don't want to cripple you,' she retorted.

'You wouldn't get the chance,' he answered, very quietly. 'But you can try.'

'Do you always use violence on women?' she demanded.

'Only ones like you—who ask for it.'

'You're a brute!'

'Possibly. Have I hit you?'

'Not yet. But I wouldn't put anything past you.' He freed her suddenly, and stood there facing her.

'I've never struck a woman in my life.' His voice was calm—and deadly.

'It doesn't stop you grabbing hold of them, though, does it?' She rubbed her arms where he had held her.

'I'm testing you, that's all.'

'What for? You've already made it clear that *my* function here is strictly as nursemaid, cook, and bottlewasher—and that *you're* the big tough hero who's going to do all the action. Big deal!' she laughed derisively, saw his face change, moved—but too late.

And this time there was no escape, none at all. This time, when he held her, it was different. For one arm was around her, crushing her, and with the other he cupped her face. Then he kissed her deeply and savagely—and satisfyingly, as she had never been kissed before.

His eyes were dark, his voice harsh. 'Now, shut up,' he said. He moved away from her, turned his back on her, and walked out of the kitchen. She stood there, too dazed to move, too stunned with the sheer *assault* to even make a sound for several moments. She heard him pick up the telephone and dial, heard his deep voice after a few moments, and pulled herself away from the cooker. To her horror she found that she was shaking. But all the fire had gone. She felt drained of all temper, of all emotion. Except one—she felt fear. Fear of this strange, disturbing, unpredictable man.

Very slowly and carefully she began to beat the eggs for her omelette. She didn't look round when he came back in the room. She didn't want to speak to him, or look at him. She was aware of him, standing just inside the doorway, watching her, yet she gave no indication that she knew he was there. Very carefully she put the finished omelette on a plate and on to the table.

'I'm going to bed,' he said.

She didn't look up. She began to eat. He walked out, closing the door after him. Tamsin looked up then. The door was all blurred, and she wiped the tears away, then began to eat.

She awoke early the next morning, lay for a moment wondering where she was, then remembered. Quickly she leapt out of bed, put on her warm blue dressing gown, and went in to look at the still sleeping children. The door of the third bedroom was ajar, but she didn't even glance in there. The arrogant male chauvinist pig who had arrived last night, and proceeded to take over, could sleep as long as he liked. Tamsin had more important tasks than seeing to his welfare. She had the children to look after; that was the reason she had come. 'He can go and take a running jump at himself,' she told the bathroom mirror in a fierce whisper as she combed her rebellious mane of black curly hair. He believed in spreading himself around, she decided, looking at the shelf by the washbasin. Aftershave lotion, shaving brush, razor, toothbrush and paste were neatly set out, almost filling the shelf. She moved them along and set out her own toiletries. Then she gave a satisfied nod and went downstairs. He had started as he meant to go on. So would she. She put on the kettle, then opened the curtains to a cold watery sun. There was a large tree-filled garden, slightly overgrown, but surrounded by high bushes and shrubs so that it apppeared, from where she stood, to be completely private. Good; the children would at least be able to play out. Tamsin was a great believer in fresh air for children—and adults—and often took her nieces and nephews for long walks on the common near their home in Cheshire.

She hummed a little song to herself as she made toast and coffee. The incident—the humiliating incident—with Blaise Torran was almost erased from her mind. She was not a girl to dwell on negative thoughts. She didn't particularly like men; she certainly didn't like *him*, but it wasn't going to affect the way she did her work over the next few weeks, that was certain.

Switching on the gas fire, she sat in front of it and ate her breakfast. It was past seven, and not a sound came from upstairs. So much for his getting up early! She finished eating, unbolted the back door, and went outside with some bread for the birds. The grass was wet still from the previous night's rain, and droplets shimmered on the leaves of the trees, and distantly a bird trilled its morning song. It was peaceful and beautiful, and Tamsin stood still, breaking up the bread and scattering it round on the grass, happy with the world. Until...

'What the hell—oh, it's you.' His voice shattered the calm. She turned, wiped the crumbs from her hands, and went towards the door where he stood waiting, hair dishevelled, tired and disgustingly unshaven.

'Good morning,' she said coolly. 'Shall I make you a coffee, or are you going to shave first?' Her tone implied—ever so gently—that he looked a sight, and it was quite intentional. She brushed past him and went over to the cooker.

'I'll have a coffee, please.'

'Black, no sugar, right? That should wake you up.' She smiled gently, infuriatingly, because she had seen herself in the mirror and perhaps he hadn't.

He sat down at the table and rubbed his stubbly face. He tried to conceal a yawn, but didn't succeed, and Tamsin, who was feeling completely wide awake, lifted her eyebrows. 'Dear me, perhaps you'd better have something to eat. Toast, bacon and eggs?'

'Just coffee will do,' he glared at her. 'If it's not too much trouble.' He didn't bother to hide the sarcasm.

'No trouble,' she said smoothly. 'I told you, I'm always up early——'

'So you did. Good for you,' he answered sourly. 'Pity they don't give medals for it.'

She made the coffee and put it on the table in front of him. 'There,' she said. 'Drink up. Some people need more sleep than others——'

He muttered something she didn't quite catch into his coffee, but she didn't ask him to repeat it. Something told her it might be wiser not to know.

'If that's all you need, I'll go and get dressed,' she said. 'Shall I wake the children?'

'No, leave them to sleep. After I've had this I'm going to look around outside——'

'There's a garage at the side of the house,' she interrupted him. 'You can put your car there. And the garden is completely surrounded by shrubs and trees, not overlooked from the road, and there are no houses anywhere near, from what I've seen anyway, and there's a front gate that closes if necessary.'

He looked at her. The look said it all. She smiled brightly, reading what was so transparently clear in his face. 'I've been trained to observe,' she said. 'It's part of my job—that's why I'm here.' On that stunning exit line, she sailed gracefully out of the kitchen, leaving him to his thoughts. She was quite sure they wouldn't be beautiful ones.

Five minutes later, dressed in warm trews and figure-hugging yellow sweater, she went down again to the kitchen. He was making himself more coffee as she went in. For a moment she was able to observe him unseen as he concentrated on pouring the boiling water into his cup. Dressed in black silky dressing gown he was indeed a powerful-looking figure of a man, tough, rough-looking—clearly not in the sunniest of moods. Tamsin felt almost sorry for him at that moment. It happened, some people were not at their best in the mornings. Her father was one. Tamsin kept well out of his way at home until he had eaten, and drunk at least three cups of strong tea. And Blaise Torran was clearly in the same league.

She began humming a catchy pop tune to herself and filled the washing up bowl with hot water from the tap, swishing in the washing up liquid as she did so. Then in went the plates from the previous evening's meal with a satisfactory clatter. She wiped the table around him, and moved the salt and pepper pots, singing softly all the while.

He sat there drinking his coffee and she wondered to herself if he would explode or merely continue simmering. It was an interesting experiment. She felt quite detached about it all, like an observer at an operation——

'Damn it! Do you have to sing?' he burst out.

'I'm sorry!' she looked at him in concern. 'Do you have a headache? I've got some Disprin upstairs——'

'No, I haven't. Hell, all I want to do is drink my coffee in peace.'

'Then you shall.' She became very quiet, swishing the plates in the water with the minimum of noise. 'There, is that better?' He didn't reply, and she sighed gently. 'Why don't you go back to bed for a while?' she suggested brightly. 'I'll introduce myself to the children when they wake up, and you can lie in until you feel——'

He stood up and put his cup down on the sink. 'I'm here to work as well, remember?' he said. 'I'm going to get washed now. I'll be down in ten minutes.'

'Don't hurry. Everything's under control——' but he'd gone. She smiled to herself. One point to me, I think, she said mentally. Which makes us quits for last night. It was still only seven-thirty. Tamsin switched on her portable radio quietly, and dried the dishes as she listened to the music flowing out.

Then she went into the living room, drew back the curtains, and built a fire, ready to light when the children were awake. There was no fireguard; she made a mental note of that. It was essential with two six-year-olds in the house. She picked up her bag, found a notepad, and began to make a list of essential items for Blaise Torran to buy. At the top of the list she wrote 'Fireguard', underlined it, then went to check all the food needed.

He came down while she was still writing at the kitchen table. She looked up, prepared to tell him about the fireguard, looked, and was silent. She had not seen him properly before, not in daylight. The grumpy bear who had sat in the kitchen bore no resemblance to this man. He wore tight black corduroy jeans and a fawn cashmere sweater. Tall, broadshouldered, clean-shaven and with his strong black hair brushed back, he was devastatingly attractive. All man, but with a certain tough elegance that caused her heart to leap. His mouth, wide and sensual, straight nose, dark, dark eyes under thick level brows, added up to a face that held touches of arrogance, cruelty— and something more—not charm exactly; it was more than that. The fleeting expression she had seen was gone, wiped away in an instant as he stared hard at her. Then she knew what it was, even as he spoke. It was virility. He possessed that quality that few men ever had, but most desired. It was an almost blatant sexuality. But not for me, she thought. You kissed me once. You won't get near enough again——

'Making a list?' he said. 'Don't forget to add candles. We might have a power cut.'

'Right.' Briskly she wrote it down. 'The most important item is a fireguard. There isn't one.' She was back to normal again. Just for a moment she had been frightened of him—the same feeling she had had the previous night after the kiss. And now she knew why.

'Yes, that is important. I might have to go further afield for one—I shouldn't imagine this one-horse village has an ironmonger's. You're to lock all doors when I'm gone and not answer to anyone. We make that a rule now and it won't get forgotten.'

It was eminently sensible. If only he could give his orders in a milder tone—she nodded. 'Of course, as you say. Then hadn't we better have a signal of knocks for when you return? I'd hate to lock *you* out.'

He looked sharply at her. 'You'll know. You'll hear the car, won't you?'

'I'm not going to spend all my time at the window looking for my car,' she pointed out. 'Just knock four times, something like that. I may be upstairs working, or in the kitchen. I'll hear you—I did last night.'

'Very well,' he nodded. 'I'm going to put my car in. Hadn't you better move yours first? It is rather in the way.'

Tamsin stood up, picked up her keys and walked out. He had the ability to make her hackles rise in no time at all, and she decided that the best thing to do would be ignore him as much as possible. Difficult, she knew, for Tamsin herself had a glorious temper when roused. And one thing was certain: he had a worse one!

She skilfully manoeuvred her Mini away from the front of the cottage and waited, turning round slightly to watch Blaise Torran put his car in the garage. When he had done so and locked the doors, she backed to where he stood.

'Right?' she asked. 'Can I leave it here?'

He gave her an odd look. 'It's not in the way.'

'No,' she got out, 'but I didn't want you to order me to move it again, you see.' And she smiled sweetly.

'A hedgehog,' he said suddenly, and clicked his fingers.

She stared at him. Was he really mad? 'What?'

'That's what you remind me of—a hedgehog. A prickly little creature, always on the defensive——'

She stalked into the house, head in the air. Because if she'd stayed outside she would very probably have hit him. Then she forgot everything, even him, at the sight which greeted her. Two small children, flaxen hair tousled with sleep, clothes rumpled, both clutching dolls, were walking down the stairs towards her.

She smiled. 'Hello. You must be Peter and Paula. I'm Tamsin.' And from behind her came Blaise Torran's deep voice. 'Hello, kids, so you're awake at last.' He stepped past Tamsin and held out his arms.

The two children hurled themselves upon him. 'Uncle Blaise,' cried the girl, 'where are we? Why isn't Mummy here?' Tamsin's heart sank. There was a trace of tears in that little-girl voice.

'Hey, up you come.' He swung her up, then turned to Tamsin, holding her tightly. 'Tamsin, my niece Paula—and this is my nephew Peter. Children, say hello.'

Nobody had told her. No one. And she had assumed—stunned, she said hello again, and in her mind was the one thought—then he must be their mother's brother. Somehow it explained quite a few things. But it also left several questions.

CHAPTER THREE

It was quiet. Blaise Torran had gone out bearing Tamsin's list, and Tamsin sat in the kitchen and watched the children spooning up their porridge. She was playing it by ear. Too much fuss, and the children would retreat into their shell. Too little, and they might start fretting for their vanished uncle.

'Right,' said Tamsin briskly as the plates were almost empty. 'Your uncle didn't say what you drank with your breakfast and I forgot to ask. Is it milk?'

Paula, the younger by eleven months, regarded her solemnly, then shook her head. 'No. We have a cup of tea.'

'Tea?' Tamsin gave a pleased smile. 'That's good. I was hoping you'd say that—it gives me an excuse to make one for myself. Now I'll let you put your own milk and sugar in because I don't know how much you have, and you'll have to help me until I get the hang of it, won't you?'

Paula nodded. She was the more confident of the two, and apparently a sensible little girl. 'I'll get the cups,' she said, scrambling off her stool as Tamsin watched the kettle boil. 'How much milk do *you* have—um—I've forgotten your name,' she confessed in a whisper.

'Tamsin Douglas. I'd like you to call me Tamsin, if you want to.'

'Tammy,' said Peter suddenly, and Paula echoed it.

'Tammy.' They both giggled, and then Tamsin was giggling with them.

'All right, Tammy it is. Just a little milk, and one sugar. Okay, can you manage the sugar, Paula?'

'Mmm, yes. Are you and Uncle Blaise going to look after us?'

'Yes, just for a little while. I've got some nieces and nephews of my own, so before I came I asked them for some games. I hope you like games, do you?'

Paula nodded. 'Oh yes. Mummy plays lots of things with us. And she takes us for our lessons as well.'

'That's good. I've just remembered, my sister-in-law put some Ladybird and Dr Seuss books in a bag. Now I don't suppose you can read very well yet——'

'Course we can!' interrupted Peter with a wide-eyed stare. 'Can't we, Paula?'

'You *can*?' Tamsin managed to show great astonishment. 'You mean you can both *read*?'

Her obvious surprise had the desired result. They both glowed with importance and pleasure. Paula nodded. 'We'll read to you if you like.'

'I'd love it! Here, drink your tea, then we'll tidy away the pots and then we'll have a reading session, and I'll see how good you are, won't I?'

It was going well—so far. Tamsin fully intended it to carry on the same. It would be work, it wouldn't be easy, but she was determined that both children would be well looked after not only materially but mentally while she had charge of them.

They all cleared away the dishes and then Tamsin went to the lounge to fetch the games and books. She spread them on the table and watched their reaction. She wasn't disappointed. Both examined the games and books with obvious pleasure and interest, little chubby fingers exploring the boxes with care.

'Okay?' She nodded. 'I'll put them away for now, and we'll sit down here, and you can read to me from a book. Pick one each that you'd like and I'll stack the others on that shelf in the corner.

Paula picked a Dr Seuss book, and Peter a Ladybird, and they all sat down. 'Ladies first,' said Tamsin. 'Off you go.'

Her attention wandered, not unnaturally, while Paula, tongue at corner of mouth, and one finger tracing the lines, began to read slowly and carefully from the book. She wondered how long Blaise Torran would be. It was so peaceful without him. On the other hand, he might well be totally different with the children around. They were clearly fond of him, and he of them, not surprisingly if he was their uncle. It would be interesting to see.

'That was fine, Paula,' she said, when at last the girl looked up. 'Very good indeed. Now, Peter, off you go.'

It was during Peter's very solemn rendition of a story about a sly old wolf that there came four resounding knocks at the front door.

'That's your uncle,' said Tamsin. 'Carry on reading, I'll not be a minute.'

Blaise Torran stood at the front door loaded with boxes of provisions, newspapers, and a fireguard. 'Wait,' he said quietly, as Tamsin picked up a box and started moving away, 'how are you getting on with them?'

'Fine.' She gave him a surprised look as if astounded that he even needed to ask. 'Just fine. We're reading in the kitchen at the moment.' And she walked away and left him standing there.

It was different. The minute he went into the kitchen, the atmosphere changed. He filled it with life, with a vibrant force that was, quite simply, part of his personality.

'Okay, kids,' he said, ruffling their hair, and they looked up giggling, delighted, 'what have you been up to?'

'We're reading to Tammy,' Paula announced, as Tamsin filled the kettle.

'Tammy?' he queried, and looked at her.

She smiled. 'That's my name from now on. We voted on it.'

'I see.' One eyebrow lifted gently. 'Then Tammy it is.'

'Coffee?' she asked him.

'Please.' He sat down at the table and picked up the book Paula had been reading. 'Hmm, I didn't know I had such clever nieces and nephews. You brought these books?' He looked at Tamsin.

'Yes. And games, and drawing paper. There'll be lots to do.'

'So I see.' He nodded as if she had done something quite surprising, and Tamsin passed him his coffee. She couldn't help it. She knew she shouldn't, but she couldn't help herself. She smiled gently at him.

'I *enjoy* looking after children. I've several nieces and nephews of my own, so I know what they like.' There was nothing in the words themselves, nothing the children would be able to detect, but he knew.

He looked at her, and she saw the response in his eyes, the awareness of the subtle undercurrents that flowed between them. 'And I'm sure you're very good at it,' he answered, very mildly. Then: 'Have you made your beds, children?' A brief, shocked silence.

'Hmm, I see you haven't. Off you go then. Neatly now—or else!' he raised his fist and frowned severely, and they laughed as they scampered out of the room. He looked at Tamsin. 'Clever, aren't you?'

'What *do* you mean?' But she smiled, because she knew.

'Don't give me that innocent wide-eyed look,' he responded. 'You know damn well what I mean. It's not what you say, it's the way that you say it.'

She shook her head. 'You're very touchy.'

'Like hell I am! You're not too old for a good spanking, and one of these days I'll give you one!'

'Violence again! Drink your coffee, it might soothe your nerves.'

He looked at her, and she stopped. That look would have stopped a tank in its tracks. Then he nodded. 'That's better. Just remember what I said. We don't fight in front of them.'

'I wasn't. *You* started it.'

'I've never met a woman,' he spoke slowly and calmly, which in an odd way only served to give his words more impact, 'who could infuriate me as much as you do in such a short time——'

'Snap!' she cut in. 'Same here. *You're* the most arrogant, bossy beast I've ever met—and I've met quite a few in my line of work.'

He stood up, and for one dreadful moment she thought he was going to strike her. 'No——' she began, and he laughed harshly.

'Don't worry—I might be tempted, but you're safe.' He smiled slowly. 'At least, while they're around.' He walked out of the room, and she heard him calling them from the foot of the stairs. 'Hurry up, it doesn't take all day!'

Tamsin was shaken. In just a few words, it had happened again. There was an explosive quality in the air whenever they were in the same room for more than a few moments, an awareness of each other, a thread of tension stretching tautly between them— and nothing they could do about it. Because it was there, that was all. She sat at the table and began to drink her coffee, and Blaise Torran walked soft-footed into the room and picked up his own cup.

He didn't speak; she didn't speak. But she could not look at him. The silence grew, and she hoped the children would come down, but there was no sound, only faint, distant giggling from upstairs. The coffee was hot, and she kept her eyes firmly fixed on the open Ladybird book, and waited.

'Lost your tongue?'

She looked up then. 'No. I've nothing to say to you.'

He smiled. He looked completely different when he smiled. 'Perhaps you're learning.'

'Learning something from *you*? I doubt it. There's nothing you could teach me.'

'Isn't there?' he enquired softly. 'We'll see, won't we?'

Tamsin looked down again at the book as if bored. 'Save your riddles for the children,' she said. 'I can't be bothered working them out.'

'It shouldn't be too difficult, even for you. I'm going to tame you, one way or another, before we leave this place.'

'Is that a threat?'

'No. A statement of fact.'

There was a clatter of feet on the stairs, voices coming nearer, and the children burst into the kitchen. And as if by magic, the electric tension vanished. She could breathe again. But she found that her hand was clenched tightly round the cup, and she couldn't help it. She heard Blaise talking to the children, and it all washed over her as if from a great distance, because for the first time in her life Tamsin was in a situation where she felt confused. Normally totally in command of her life—since the disaster at nineteen, about which she still refused to think—she had always known exactly where she was with people. Yet with this man she was no longer sure.

She suddenly realised she was being spoken to. She hadn't heard a word. 'Sorry?' They were waiting, looking at her.

Blaise Torran's voice was almost gentle. How swiftly he could switch from arrogance to calm! 'I was telling the children that we're going to have a lot of fun while we're here—aren't we, Tammy?' No undercurrents there—at least none she could detect.

She nodded. 'Oh yes, we are. There's a super large garden at the back—I know lots of games we can play, and if it's raining—well, we've got books and games and television.' She smiled at them, and Paula came over and hugged her impulsively.

'I *like* you,' she declared. 'I won't mind being away from Mummy for a wee while just as long as you're here.' She turned to her uncle while Tamsin smiled, unsure, for a moment, whether she wanted to laugh or cry. 'Do you like Tammy, Uncle?' she demanded.

Oh, *no*, Tamsin wanted to call, you shouldn't have asked that!

He laughed. 'Of course I do!' The dark eyes dared her to call him a liar. 'We're going to get on splendidly.'

Then came the question that she supposed she had
sensed, subconsciously, all along. It was Peter who
spoke. He had been regarding them both with a serious expression. He talked less than his extrovert sister,
but clearly he thought a lot. 'Are you and Tammy
going to get married, Uncle?' he said.

Only by a supreme effort of will did Tamsin control
herself from breaking into hysterical laughter. Marry
him! 'Why, no, Peter,' said Blaise, very calm, very
reasoned, 'we don't know one another very well at all.
And you only marry people you've known for a while.'

'But why are you both looking after us if you don't
know each other?' Peter persisted. Clearly not a child
to be sidetracked, and Tamsin waited with quiet
amusement to see the man's response.

'It just so happened that your mummy knew I had a
holiday, and thought it would be nice for me to bring
you with me, and it also happened that she knows
Tammy's father, and mentioned it to him—and he
said, how nice, Tammy's got a holiday and nowhere
particular to go, and they knew of this cottage, so it
seemed a nice idea for us all to have a holiday together, you see?' As a fairy story, thought Tamsin,
bemused, it was beautiful. You couldn't fault it. She
almost began to believe it herself. What a skilful liar he
was!

Paula chipped in. 'I wish you would get married.
I'd like to be a bridesmaid. I've *never* been a bridesmaid, it's not fair!'

'You're only young,' said Tamsin. 'I wasn't a
bridesmaid until I was ten. How old are you—six?'

'Yes. You'd look awfully pretty in a long white
dress, Tammy—wouldn't she, Uncle? Don't you
think she's very pretty?' They could start a match-

making agency, she and her brother, thought Tamsin, any time at all.

'Indeed I do,' Blaise responded valiantly. It was difficult to see whether he was amused or annoyed. His expression gave nothing away.

'Are you going to kiss her?' asked Paula, who had put her thumb in her mouth and was regarding them both with frank interest. Tamsin's cup nearly went flying, and she rescued it swiftly. Please let me escape, she thought, before I burst out laughing. How could he cope with *that*?

'I hadn't thought about it,' he answered smoothly. 'It's not very nice to go around kissing ladies you hardly know, is it?'

True, thought Tamsin. Very true, but it didn't stop *you*. 'Tammy wouldn't mind, would you, Tammy?' said Paula, fixing her with friendly, innocent blue eyes.

'Well, I——' Tamsin was confused. The glint in Blaise Torran's eyes didn't help. 'I'm not sure. As your uncle said, I don't really know him.' And to forestall the next, inevitable question from these two frank children, she added hastily: 'Even though he is very nice, and I do like him.' And may you be forgiven for that lie, she thought.

Paula sighed happily. 'So we all like each other. I think that's *lovely*, don't you, Peter?'

'I don't always like *you*,' he answered. 'You pinched my Action Man last week——'

'I didn't! You fibber! You said I could borrow it——'

'Only for ten minutes, and you had it *all* day——'

Tamsin escaped to the sink, leaving them arguing. Let Uncle Blaise sort that one out, she'd had enough.

'Okay, that's it, kids. No fighting! Now we're going to light a fire and try that fireguard out while Tammy clears away, so come with me.' And he took each one by the hand and led them out of the room.

Tamsin let out her breath in a long, beautiful sigh of relief. 'Phew!' Her training hadn't prepared her for that little scene. She filled a cup with water and drank it thirstily. Those dear little children! What next? she thought. Had she really imagined a pleasant, simple little job? No cares, no problems, play games, read a book, draw—they were like a couple of detectives themselves——

'I've left them watching a schools programme on television.' Blaise's voice from nearby—too near, and she started. 'Out of the mouths of babes——' he smiled gently as she whirled round.

'But you tell such lovely fairy stories,' she responded sweetly. 'You nearly brought a tear to my eye.'

'Yes, I'll bet I did. So we all love one another. Isn't that nice?'

'As long as you don't pinch my Action Man,' she retorted smartly.

He laughed, genuinely amused. 'Quick-witted too. Hmm,' he nodded. 'That makes it more interesting.'

'Makes *what* more interesting?' she asked.

'Why, the taming of Tamsin, that's what,' was the swift answer. 'No use taming a creature with no fight in it.'

'You're not at the circus now,' she shot back. 'I'm sure you fancy yourself as a lion tamer or something, but I don't respond to whips and chains!'

'You're a woman,' he interrupted, 'I know *that*. My methods will be more subtle.'

'Like kissing by force?' she shot back. 'Oh yes, that's *very* subtle. You're a real smoothie—I don't think!' Her eyes sparkled, her cheeks were pink, and she saw the subtle change in his expression—and she turned away quickly. She had seen that look on men's faces before, and she hated it. She hated men, come to that, ever since Nigel—she hated them all——

'Don't turn away,' he said softly. 'I like it when you look mad. It only makes me the more determined.'

'I'll turn away from you if I want,' she shot back. 'You don't own me, and you never will.' She kept her back resolutely to him. He would not dare to touch her, not with the children so near.

'Won't I?' he said quietly. 'Perhaps not. But I may make love to you before you're much older.'

'You?' she whirled round then. 'You won't get the chance!'

He didn't say anything, but he smiled. That was enough—it was more than enough. Tamsin hit him hard, before he could guess her intent. She struck him so hard across his face that it jerked his head to one side. And she didn't care. It was what she had wanted to do, had known she would do, ever since the first moment she had seen him. She watched the mark fade on his cheek, and still he didn't move, and that was more frightening than if he had grabbed hold of her. She took a deep, shaky breath as she realised suddenly what she had done. Why didn't he move, speak, do something—anything?

Then he did. 'That,' he said, 'makes it even more interesting.' He turned away and walked out of the room, leaving her alone. And she was left with the memory of a fleeting expression she had seen on his face. Now she knew what was to happen. It had all been there, just for one fraction of a second. He was a man who always did what he said he would, and for that instant of time she had seen the naked desire in his eyes.

She gripped the sink tightly, to stop herself from falling. What had her father said? That he was a woman-hater? But he was more of a man than any she had met, and that was the most frightening fact of all. Dear God, she thought, the children are here, and while they are about, I am safe. But there are also the long evening hours, when they're asleep. And the night. Many nights, sleeping here in a house with him, and he has said what he has said—and he means it.

'Can I have a glass of milk, please? Uncle said I was to ask you.'

Tamsin looked down to see Paula standing there, smiling. 'Of course you may, love. Here.' Her hands weren't quite steady as she filled a glass with milk from the refrigerator. 'Doesn't Peter want one?'

'No. He's watching television, but I got bored. Can I stay with you?'

That gave Tamsin the idea, and she gave the little girl a beaming smile. 'Of course you can. I'm just tidying up. Sit down and watch me if you like.' Of course. It was a beautiful idea and so simple. 'I've been thinking,' she said. 'How would you like me to move my bed into your room? Then, if you wake up in the night and want anything, I'll be there.'

Paula nodded, and finished the milk, leaving a white moustache above her mouth. 'Mmm, lovely,' she said. 'Shall we go and do it now, or ask Uncle Blaise to help?'

'Why not now?' Tamsin took her hand. 'Let's surprise him, hey?'

They ran up the stairs, giggling like a couple of children, and into Tamsin's room. Her heart sank. The bed was very heavy and old.

Paula frowned. 'Do you think we're strong enough?' she asked, with all the direct logic of the six-year-old.

'I don't know, love,' admitted Tamsin. 'Oh dear——' she stopped.

'It's all right, I'll go and ask——' and before Tamsin could stop her, the child had gone.

'Wait——' said Tamsin, but too late. She heard voices, then Paula came running up again.

'He says he can't,' she announced. 'He's got a bone in his leg. What does he mean, Tammy?'

Tamsin smiled grimly. 'It means,' she said, 'that he doesn't feel strong enough to move anything today.' She sighed. I can imagine the comments now, she thought wryly. And I'll have asked for them. 'Come on, we'll go down. I'll sort something out later.' There was a lock on the door, and a key in the lock, but she couldn't lock herself in for fear they cried out and she didn't hear. She took a last look at the key, and then went downstairs. Her brain was working overtime.

It was after tea that Tamsin went up to her room again, and the first thing she noticed was that the key had gone. For a moment she stood still. Had she imagined seeing one there? She went over and touched the lock, and a sense of fear washed over her. She hadn't imagined it. There had been one, and now it was gone. And there was only one person who would have taken it.

The children were watching a comedy show, sprawled on cushions on the floor laughing, while Blaise read the morning paper. He had washed up after their meal, had put more coal on the fire, which blazed merrily, and now sat as if he hadn't a care in the world. Tamsin watched him from the door, and he looked up, and saw what was in her eyes. He rose to his feet, putting the paper down, and Tamsin walked out to the kitchen.

She turned on him as he went in. 'Where is it?' she demanded.

'Where is what?'

'You know damn well——'

'Don't raise your voice to me, I'm not deaf.'

'The key, damn you!'

'What key?' Insolent amusement in his eyes made her more furious than she already was.

'To my bedroom door.'

'Oh, *that* one.'

'Yes, *that* one. Where is it?'

'I took it,' he shrugged.

'I know damn well you did. Why? I want it back.'

'Because it's not safe to be locked in at night. In case of fire——'

'It's a damn sight safer to be locked in than worrying about what you're up to!' she snapped.

'Really? What do you think I'd be up to?'

'You don't want me to spell it out, do you?'

'I think you'd better.' He was infuriatingly calm. 'You don't imagine I'm going to come sneaking into your room?'

'The thought had crossed my mind, yes,' she retorted.

'And do you think I'd chance your screaming, and waking the kids?'

'I don't know what you'd chance. I don't know you,

do I?' she shot back. 'Except that you're over-sexed——'

'What?' he looked almost amused. 'What makes you say that?'

She was tired of the verbal fencing. 'Give it to me!'

He smiled. 'Oh, I'll give it to you all right—one day.'

'The key!'

He lifted one eyebrow. 'Isn't that what we were talking about?'

'*I* was. *You* seem to be going off at a tangent.'

'Tut, tut, Tammy, you really must get over this obsession of yours about sex. It's not natural for a young girl like you to be so worried.'

'After what *you* said? You must be joking!'

'What did I say?' He seemed to genuinely want to know.

'I shouldn't need to remind you. Unless, of course, you automatically assume every female wants to leap into bed with you at the first opportunity—or you proposition all the women you meet——'

'I don't.'

'How do *I* know that?'

'I've just told you, that's how.'

'Huh! And you're the biggest liar I've ever met——'

'Because I told the kids I liked you? I didn't have much choice. They've seen enough battles in their young lives.'

'I didn't mean that!'

'What did you mean?'

But she was beginning to feel very confused. The subject of the key seemed to have been neatly side-stepped—and she didn't know how. 'I want the key back,' she said. 'My key.' She was shaking with a mixture of anger and helplessness. And he knew. That was what made it worse. He *knew*.

'No,' he said. 'I can't allow it. If there was a fire——'

'You've already said that—and anyway, judging by the state you're in in the morning, I shouldn't think you'd be much use at waking anyone up—you probably sleep like a log.'

'Then I'm hardly likely to go around raping you in the middle of the night,' he pointed out.

Tamsin's answer was short and to the point. 'Get lost!' She whirled away from him, too furious to think clearly, and he laughed.

'Why do you hate men so?' he asked.

She caught her breath, shocked. Wordlessly, she looked out of the window, seeing the image of Nigel's face, as it had been once—and tears filled her eyes.

'Why?' he repeated, and turned her round, and saw her face before she could blot out the memories. She felt rather than heard his indrawn breath. She looked at him.

'Leave me alone,' she said in a whisper. 'Just—leave me alone.'

'Someone hurt you.' He said it, and it wasn't a question. And his tone wasn't mocking or sarcastic; she could not have borne that. His voice was almost gentle—almost.

A tear trickled down her cheek, and she tasted the saltiness on her lips. She shook her head. 'Please,' she said.

Blaise let her go. Then, without another word, he had left the kitchen, and she was alone. Very carefully

Tamsin poured milk into a pan for the children's Horlicks. Her anger had evaporated, and she felt instead a numbness spreading through her. She had seen many expressions on Blaise Torran's face, but until that moment when he had held her briefly, and seen the pain in her eyes, she had not seen one expression. Now she had, and it was in a way more disturbing than the others. For she had seen compassion. She didn't want that from anybody, but particularly not from him. Not from him.

CHAPTER FOUR

THE next day was Sunday, and normally Tamsin slept a little later. Instead, because of a restless, dream-filled night, she was awake before six, and lay for a few minutes thinking over all that happened the previous day. She looked at her door. When she had gone to bed she had wedged it open a few inches with a chair. Wide enough for her to hear a child call; not wide enough for anyone to come in without making a great clatter, due to the metal vase she had delicately balanced on the tilted chair back. It was still in place. But her mind had been in a turmoil, and she had paid for it in little sleep, and that nightmarish. She felt grey and depressed.

She knew she would not sleep again. The children would not wake for a while—and neither would Blaise, not if he kept up the previous morning's form. Tamsin decided she would go for a walk. She washed and dressed and went downstairs to the cold quiet house. For a moment or two she stood in the kitchen looking out of the windows, then, shrugging, she put on her coat, found her key, and went out of the front door. It was still dark, and cold, but crisp with frost, and the air sharp to the lungs, and she knew which direction she must take, towards the village. Twenty minutes would be sufficient, and then she would return, have an early breakfast, and do some washing.

And then what? The rest of the day seemed to stretch ahead, with one person dominant; Blaise Torran. Always it came back to him, as if he were the core of all that troubled her. And yet he wasn't, Tamsin knew that. And now he knew something too. He had seen it in her eyes, and while he couldn't know exactly what it was, he had said the three words that she had never wanted to hear from anybody. 'Someone hurt you.'

She dug her hands deep into her pockets. 'No,' she said fiercely, as if that might erase the words. 'No!' She began to run along the rutted track, her feet sure in the semi-darkness, swift and light-footed. The run had the desired effect. When she slowed at last, she was breathless and rosy-cheeked, her heart pounding with the added exertion. And she was ready to go back. She turned and began to walk towards the house again. She was out of sight of it, the narrow track surrounded on both sides by trees, dark and shadowy and silent because even the birds were still abed. Like all sensible people, she told herself. The thought of a cup of coffee in a warm kitchen, with perhaps a piece of hot crunchy buttery toast, made her mouth water in anticipation. Then she would catch up on yesterday's newspapers.

But then she saw the car. It was hidden, parked behind some trees, just off the road, and she wouldn't have seen it then, only that there had been a brief flicker of light from behind steamy windows, as though someone had just lit a cigarette. She stopped, stared hard, and she wasn't afraid. She hadn't seen the car on her way out—but had its occupants seen her? Nothing moved. There was no sound—and the car was only twenty yards away from the gate of the cottage. She stood very still and watched, then heard a slight movement, as though someone were about to open a door.

She had to tell Blaise. Alone, she could do nothing—she ran, faster than she had ever run in her life before, along the road, up the path, key in door—lock it behind her, then up the stairs and into his room. He slept, gloriously and utterly, flat on his back, dead to the world. Tamsin shook him roughly. 'Wake up! Blaise—*wake up!*'

Something of her urgency must have reached him, for he stirred, looked at her blearily, muttered something, and tried to push her hand away. She knelt by the bed, knowing she must not wake the children as well. 'There's a car parked just outside,' she whispered. 'Wake *up*—please wake *up!*'

And instantly, miraculously, he was awake. He sat up. 'What?'

'There's a car—I went for a walk—Blaise, someone's in it, and it's so near the house. Do you think——'

'Close your eyes.' He was pushing back the bedclothes and she hastily closed her eyes. She heard a belt buckle being fastened and risked opening them again to see him nearly dressed, pulling on a dark sweater and feeling for his shoes at the same time.

'Where?'

'Outside the gate—turn left—in the trees——'

'Okay. Lock the door after me, and don't open it to anyone, only me.'

He was out of the door, and she ran after him down the stairs. 'Wait, let me——'

He turned on her. 'Stay here. If I'm not back in fifteen minutes get the police, okay?'

'But there might be more than——'

'Yes, there might. If anyone tries to get in, dial 999. Now, lock it.' And he was gone. Tamsin's vivid imagination did the rest. She clasped her hands together in a torment of indecision. She should not have let him go alone. And yet it was obvious that the children could not be left. Suppose he was attacked? Suppose ... She looked at the telephone and back towards the front door. Then she looked at her watch. Six-thirty. Fifteen minutes, he had said. Fifteen. She ran up the stairs and took a look in at the sleeping children, then she ran down and into the kitchen where she put on the kettle. Twelve minutes. The kettle boiled and she switched it off. Nine minutes ... She put her hands to her head. If only she knew what was happening! If she counted it might be better. She began to count off the seconds, and then it was eight minutes, then seven, then six, and then...

'Tammy, let me in!'

'Blaise?' Heart in mouth she ran to the door. 'Blaise? Is it you?'

'It's me, Miss Hedgehog.'

No one else could know that! Tamsin fumbled for the bolts, opened the door, and he practically fell in. Anxious, she took his arm, searching in the face for any sign of injury—and saw that he was laughing, Laughing! She couldn't believe her eyes. 'What is it?' she demanded, wide-eyed, and he looked at her.

'Lord,' he said, 'I wish you'd stayed in bed,' and he walked off towards the kitchen.

Numbly she followed. Everything had gone mad, and he particularly. Why should he laugh? What was so funny? He sat at the table, head in hands, and looked up at her, all laughter gone. 'Get me a coffee,' he said.

This was not the time to ask questions. Something, somehow, was not as it should be, but she had no idea what. Why should he laugh though? She made him coffee, and one for herself. There was silence, until she could bear it no longer, and she said, almost timidly: 'Blaise? What——'

He looked up. His eyes had been nearly closed again—in another minute, she thought, he'd have fallen asleep.

'Do me a favour,' he said. 'Don't go out for early morning walks, okay?'

'But the car—I had to tell you——' ·

'I know, I know.' He shook his head wearily. 'You did the right thing—only I went charging along, prepared to batter some sense into my brother-in-law and or his friends—and nearly got myself a black eye from a woman.'

It didn't register for a moment. Then, at last, light dawned. 'You mean——?'

'I mean that there was a couple in that car, engaged in minding their own business, and the woman had a temper like you, and took a swing at me. The man was too busy hiding his face—but it wasn't anyone I know, and in any case both had broad Yorkshire accents, which nobody, but nobody, can fake.'

Suddenly the funny side of it hit Tamsin. She began to laugh, softly at first, then more loudly, out of sheer relief from tension. Blaise looked sourly at her. 'I'm happy you're amused,' he said. 'It makes me feel better at losing a few hours' sleep.'

She sobered up. 'I'm sorry, I'm really sorry. You'd better go back to bed.'

He stood up. 'I'm going.'

She had to make up for the *faux pas* somehow. 'I'll bring you breakfast in bed later on.'

He looked at her. 'If you wish. Not before nine, okay? And don't forget to leave the door wide open when you come in, in case I decide to rape you.' He yawned and then leered blearily. 'And just as a point of interest—if I wanted to get into your bedroom at night, you don't think that crackpot idea of yours would stop me, do you?'

'What crackpot——' she began.

'The vase on the chair. Dear, dear, I've got long arms. You wouldn't hear it move, I promise you that.' He went out, leaving Tamsin puzzled and confused. How had he known? She had no intention of asking now, but she would later.

Silence fell again. She began to load the washer with clothes, then switched it on. Then she went to vacuum the living room, and prepare a fire for later that morning. At least, whatever other result had come from the fiasco of her walk, it had effectively banished her depressed mood. She felt almost cheerful as she set to work.

By eleven that morning the effects of a bad night and early morning rising had hit Tamsin. She left the children in the lounge and crept upstairs to lie down for fifteen minutes—or so she told herself. She awoke to feel Blaise Torran pulling her arm gently, and opened her eyes. 'Mmm?' she muttered.

'It's noon. You've been asleep—are you intending to stay in bed for the rest of the day?'

She sat up guiltily. 'I'm sorry—I felt a little tired, and——'

'I know. I heard you snoring very prettily as I came up.' Tamsin looked at him, horrified.

'I wasn't, was I?'

He laughed. 'No. But you were certainly out for the count.'

'I'm coming down now.'

'Stay there. I've got lunch on in the oven, the fire's going well, and the kids are playing draughts—there's no need for you to come down.'

Tamsin yawned. 'I had a rotten night's sleep. That's why I was up so early. I didn't realise it would hit me so strongly, though.'

Blaise looked at her, and for a moment her heart stood still. She wanted to look away, but she couldn't. To cover up, and to forestall what he might say, because she didn't want to hear it, she asked: 'How did you know about the chair?'

He raised one eyebrow in that infuriating way he had. 'I heard the elaborate preparations.' He shook his head. 'You'd have done better balancing the vase on top of the door instead. Only trouble is, you might have gone to the bathroom in the middle of the night and forgotten about it.' He smiled. 'So you'll just have to find a more efficient way of protecting your honour.'

Tamsin lay back in bed. 'Go away.' She closed her eyes.

'I'm going.' And he did. But she heard him laughing as he went. That decided her. She would get up right now and go down. She had hung the washing out in the garden, and with any luck it might be sufficiently dry to bring in and air, although, looking out of the window at the cold grey sky, Tamsin doubted it.

After splashing her face with cold water she was fully wide awake, and went down to see a scene of perfect domestic harmony. The two children were sitting on cushions by a good fire engrossed in draughts, and Blaise was looking through the books on a bookshelf and didn't even turn as she peeped into the lounge. Just for a moment she thought: it's like being married—and dismissed the thought as she walked briskly out to the kitchen.

The washing was stiff on the line, and far from dry. She sighed and began to unpeg it. It would be useless to leave it any longer, for although a watery sun shone, the air was cold and damp. She spread everything out over a wooden clothes horse, chanced a quick look in the oven, where something that smelt delicious was cooking in a foil-covered dish, then looked around her. There was really no work to do. Everything was tidy. So what now? she thought. Go and join them? It was the obvious answer, yet she hesitated. She switched on the radio and tuned it to Family Favourites, sat at the kitchen table, and began to write in her diary, something she tried to do daily, but didn't always manage.

'Hmm. Busy?'

She looked up. She hadn't heard him come in. He moved very quietly for all his size. 'Yes,' she answered briefly, and went on writing.

'Don't let me disturb you.'

'I won't.' She continued writing.

'I'll just prepare the vegetables,' he said. 'For our lunch.'

'I can do that, when I've finished this,' she said.

'Please don't stop. I'm sure your diary is more important than——'

'There's no need to be sarcastic,' she answered. 'You did appoint me as cook, remember? I'll do them in ten minutes when I've finished this.'

'Okay. I thought we'd have potatoes and sprouts.'

'Then that is what I shall do. Don't worry, I'll find them.' She looked up at him. 'I hope you enjoyed your breakfast in bed?'

The irony wasn't lost on him. He smiled. 'Beautiful. It's nice to be waited on occasionally.'

'Isn't it just? I'll have to try it some time.'

He pulled up a chair from the table and sat down. 'You know,' he said conversationally, 'it's just like being married, isn't it? Kiddies playing happily by the fire, Mummy in the kitchen listening to Family Favourites——'

'And Daddy, supervising the work——'

'No, Daddy getting lunch ready and putting it in the oven *all by himself*——'

'Gosh! So you did. I forgot.' She widened her eyes and stared at him in mock admiration. 'Aren't you clever!'

'Yes.' He nodded and hung his head modestly. Tamsin had had enough of the silly game. She stood up, slammed her diary shut and said:

'I'll do the vegetables now. If you want to watch, feel free.'

'I take it the idea of marriage doesn't appeal to you,' he said in conversational tones.

'Why don't you mind your own business?'

'You like children. You must do, or you wouldn't have taken this job on.'

'I could say the same about you,' she retorted smartly, keeping on the move, busily occupied in finding a potato peeler, and newspaper. Damn him, she wasn't going to get involved in a personal discussion with him.

'I'm related to them—there's the difference.'

'And you have the kind of job that just lets you take off when you feel like it? Lucky you!'

'Not exactly. I'll be working while I'm here, to be more precise.'

'Oh, don't tell me!' She turned round from the sink to stare at him. 'You're an artist! And you'll just find yourself a little old attic while you're here and go up and do your masterpieces——'

'You're getting close.' He was calm, almost amused —which in a perverse way, increased Tamsin's annoyance.

'Close? Ah, I know—a poet! That would explain the black silk dressing gown,' she began to laugh. 'You've not got all the props. You should carry a long cigarette holder and a leather-bound volume of poems under your arm——'

'And you're asking for a good spanking.'

'Not from you I'm not,' she retorted. 'What are you, then? A sculptor?'

'No. A writer.'

'Snap! I sent a little piece to our local paper once, and got two pounds. Is that what you do?'

'No. But I'll want the kitchen table in the evenings. I may work late at night. But I'll close the door, so my typewriter won't keep you awake.'

She looked at him. He wasn't joking. Then she remembered seeing the typewriter in his room, when she had taken up his breakfast. It hadn't really registered, because she had been intent on getting out as speedily as possible. She swallowed. 'You mean—you *are* a writer?'

'I thought I'd just told you.'

Tamsin couldn't help herself. She really didn't want to know what he wrote—but the question came out almost of its own volition. 'What—do you write?'

'Plays mostly.' He stood up. 'I'll go and see what the kids are doing. They're a bit too quiet.' When he was almost at the door, he turned, paused, and added: 'There's a play of mine on television tonight at ten o'clock.' And he walked out. His timing was impeccable. As an exit line it was perfect. And Tamsin stood there gaping for a moment, completely stunned.

Recovering, she picked up the paper she had found to put the peelings in, and searched through for the TV programme page. He was lying, of course—but even as she looked, she knew he wasn't. It was there, on the page, quite clearly, 'the Ten o'clock Play,' it said, *'One for the Road* by Bill Torrance.'

'Found it? I thought you might have.'

She looked up. 'B-but—I've seen his plays before——'

'*My* plays before,' he interrupted gently.

'Bill Torrance?'

'Blaise William Torran is my real name. I altered it slightly.' He gave a modest, unassuming smile. 'It saves being recognised everywhere, you know.'

'You're not kidding me, are you?'

'No, I'm not kidding you. I only told you because you asked me my job—implying, if I'm not mistaken, that I was probably some scrounger off the state——' Tamsin reddened at the accuracy of his remark, 'and because I could hardly be typing away down here night after night without arousing your curiosity.' He shrugged. 'So now you know.'

'Are you going to watch it tonight?'

'No. I never do. I'll be working. But if you want to, feel free.'

Tamsin turned away and slammed the paper down. 'I'll see. I might be reading.' It was a lie. Nothing would have prevented her watching—but she wouldn't give him the satisfaction of knowing. He laughed, as if he guessed.

'I don't care what you do.' It was obvious that he genuinely didn't. He picked up a sprout, removed the outer leaves and ate it. 'Hmm, not bad.'

'If you eat them all now, there won't be any left to cook.'

'I took one, that's all. Don't be so quick to attack, Tammy.'

'You mean like *you* are? I'll try not.'

He stood close to her and looked at her as if weighing her up. She gritted her teeth and began to peel the mound of potatoes in the bowl. 'You know,' said Blaise, 'I've had an idea.'

She ignored him, and concentrated on what she was doing.

'Don't you want to know what it is? It concerns you.'

'No.'

'I might set a play in a detective agency. I could get a lot of first-hand information from you—you know, the kind of jobs you get——'

'Why don't you try working in one for a while?'

'Oh, I've done that before—not in a detective agency I don't mean, but once, when I wanted to set a play behind the scenes in a big hotel, I went to work

in the kitchens for a month. That was an eye-opener.
And the play was on TV about a year ago. Called
Backstage, about this temperamental chef who falls for
a receptionist——'

'I saw it.' She had laughed all the way through it as
well, only she wouldn't admit that. It was one of the
best plays she had seen for a long time, and she
remembered it very vividly. It had also won a television award. Tamsin began to feel very confused.
Could this arrogant man, this almost frightening man,
really be the author of such gently witty comedy?

'Oh, you did? Well then, it's much easier, of course,
to get the background on things by actually being on
the spot. But I'm sure you can fill me in equally well
on agency work, the type of clients, their problems——'

'It's all confidential,' she said primly.

'Come off it! I'm not asking for names, just out-
lines.'

'Then why don't you ask my father?' As if on cue,
the telephone rang.

'I'll get it,' he said, and went.

He was gone so long that she thought the call must
be for him, and carried on peeling. Until he shouted
to her. 'Tammy, it's your father.' Then she knew why
he'd been talking.

She took the receiver from him. 'Hello, Dad.'

'Hello, love. Everything okay?'

'Yes, perfect.'

'Good. Well, there's a turn-up, hey? Your Mr
Torran being a playwright.'

'Yes. Has he——'

Tamsin was well aware of the man standing nearby,
which didn't make the conversation any easier. 'He's

asked me about setting a play in an agency like ours. And he also said you'd told him you couldn't possibly divulge any confidences——' She risked a brief glance at the waiting Blaise, who leant against the wall, arms folded, not quite smirking, but almost, because he was a crafty devil all right. He'd clearly managed to get round her father, who was still speaking—'which of course, he quite understood—but you know, love, he's promised to disguise everything you tell him so well that nobody would recognise——'

'You mean,' she burst out, 'I've got to tell him——'

'About some of the cases? Of course. No names—but you know the interesting ones, and he's given me his word——'

I'll bet he has, she thought. She was furious, with Blaise, with her father, and with herself, for being such a fool. 'All right,' she managed, 'I understand. You're the boss.'

There was a slight pause. Her father was a very shrewd man. 'Tam?' he said, 'what is it, love?'

They had a code for when they couldn't talk, when anyone might overhear. She said: 'You won't forget to post those letters for me, will you?'

'Aha! He's hovering nearby, is he?'

'Something like that,' she agreed mildly.

'I *see*. And do I detect a certain lack of rapport between you?'

'Well, I suppose you could say so.'

'He's not giving you trouble, is he? You know what kind I mean?'

'Heavens, no!' She gave a laugh. 'It's nothing really. Er—everything all right your end?'

'Fine. I'll ring you tomorrow, shall I?'

'Yes.' She said goodbye and hung up. 'I'll finish the

vegetables,' she said, and stalked past Blaise Torran, who began whistling softly as she passed him, then went into the lounge. It wasn't until she was in the kitchen, and hearing the same tune on the radio, that she recognised the song he had been whistling. *'Help Me Make it Through the Night.'*

Tamsin flung a peeled potato into the pan. 'Not on your life!' she muttered crossly. The cheek of him! The sheer breathtaking impudence, sweet-talking her father, no doubt giving him the full patter. She would think out some of the most incredibly *dull* cases she could remember and see if she could bore him stiff. She smiled a little smile to herself. Now that would be interesting. She wondered how boring she could possibly be if she tried really hard. It made her recall a former secretary at the office, efficient enough in her work, but quite incapable of telling any incident without constant repetition. 'It was last Tuesday—or was it Wednesday? No, wait a minute, it must have been Tuesday because that was the day I had to go to the launderette, only it was closed—it's not usually closed on a Tuesday, but the woman in charge hadn't turned up, so it was locked when I got there, so as I say, last Tuesday—where was I?' by which time anyone listening would be glassy-eyed, wondering if she would ever get to the point. Hm, thought Tamsin, and began to mentally rehearse her lines. That would teach him a lesson! But she should have known better by then.

Sunday evening, and neither her work at the agency, nor his writing, had been mentioned again. It wasn't, Tamsin thought, as if she could put her finger on anything. It wasn't as if Blaise was deliberately avoiding the subjects—more as if he had completely forgotten them. Which annoyed her, because it is one thing to prepare clever answers—it's quite another if nobody bothers to ask the questions.

He had spent a lot of time with the children, playing ball in the garden for quite a while, making them run about until they were rosy-cheeked and laughing. Tamsin had watched them for a few minutes from the kitchen window, seeing the man who both infuriated and intrigued her, as she hadn't seen him before. Running, stooping to catch the ball, his hair shaggy and uncombed, a loose dark blue suede jacket on, and laughing as he called them or dodged them. Just for an instant he had turned, as if aware of her regard, and their eyes had met, and in them she had seen something that made her tighten her mouth and turn away. It was an awareness, a knowledge—and she didn't like it. It was as if he could read her thoughts.

Then, later, when they had trooped in, breathless, eyes shining, she had made drinking chocolate for them all, and they had gone in the lounge to play one of the games. Tamsin found an iron and pressed the newly aired clothes, and wondered why she felt a sudden sense of loneliness. It was as if they had excluded her.

She prepared their tea, and afterwards, when all was cleared away and tidied, the children had telephoned their mother before going to bed. Now, at eight o'clock, Tamsin sat alone in the lounge, with the television on, a book on her knee, and listened for the sound of the typewriter from the kitchen. She was neither reading nor watching. She was, quite simply, too curious to know what Blaise was doing to concentrate on anything else. It annoyed her, but she could do nothing about it. She looked at her watch, and decided. In half an hour she would go and make coffee for herself, and for him if he wanted it. Because the decision was made she was able to read—but the next half hour passed incredibly slowly.

It was time. She walked out, confident, telling herself she was very thirsty, and it was quite natural to want a drink—and into the kitchen. The back door was wide open, the typewriter was on the table, and a stack of paper stood at one side of it. At the other a thinner pile, typewritten. But there was not a sign of Blaise. And there was no sound from outside.

CHAPTER FIVE

HEART in mouth, Tamsin ran to the door and peered out into the darkness. 'Blaise,' she called softly.

'Right. Stay there.' She heard his voice from not far away, and her heart thudded in relief. Then she saw the dark shadowy figure break away from the blackness of the trees and walk across the garden towards her.

'I wondered——' she began.

He came up the steps, bringing icy air in with him, then bolted the door and turned to her. 'I heard a noise,' he said.

'Why didn't you call me?' she asked. She filled the kettle and put it on.

'What for? I wanted to see what it was first.' He ran his fingers through his hair. 'There's nothing outside, and the gate's closed.'

'What kind of noise?'

'Crackling—as though someone was pushing a way through the trees——' Despite her courage, she felt a shiver of apprehension. The cottage was remote, with no neighbouring houses. There was no reason for anyone to be near. No good reason, that was.

'It could have been an animal,' she said.

'Quite possibly. A fairly large one, judging by the sounds.' He looked down at her. 'You're not scared, are you?'

She shook her head. 'No. Just for a moment, when you said crackling—I felt a shiver, but it passed. No, I'm not scared.' And it was true.

She saw him smile as she turned away to watch the kettle. Perhaps he didn't believe her. She didn't care—so she told herself, but she did. 'I'm making coffee,' she told him. 'Want one?'

'Yes, please—good grief, is that the time?' He flexed his fingers and sat down at the table. Tamsin was dying to know what he was writing, but she wasn't going to ask.

'If it's not a rude question, what time are you going to be out here typing until?'

He looked at her. 'Twelve—one—two—I don't know. As long as I feel like it. Why?'

'No reason. I just don't want to get a shock when I come down in the morning and see you still clattering away at the table, that's all.'

'It's hardly likely—though I did actually stay up all night, once, when I had a deadline—it's not usual, though.'

She handed him the coffee. 'Then I'll leave you to it. Will it interrupt you if I come out later—say about ten—for another coffee?'

'No.' He smiled quite charmingly. 'Then you can watch the play in peace, can't you?'

She picked up her coffee, went towards the door, turned, and said graciously: 'I'd forgotten all about that,' and went out. He wasn't the only one who could make good exits. She thought she heard him laughing, but couldn't be sure, and certainly wasn't going back to find out.

She was engrossed in the play when he came in, and

she looked up guiltily, like a child caught in the act of stealing the jam from the larder.

'Oh, I——' She wished he would *go*. She didn't want to miss a minute of it, but she could hardly say so. She wondered if her cheeks were red.

'Just came to tell you I'd had a look at the kids, and they're both asleep. I've just made coffee too. You forgot, didn't you? Want one?'

'Yes, please.' If only he'd go and leave her alone.

'Right. Won't be a minute.' He went out whistling quietly, leaving the door open. A few moments later he was back bearing a beaker. After he had handed it to her he remained standing to one side of her, and slightly behind her chair, so that she couldn't see his face—or whether he was watching her or the television. She sighed. He'd ruined it. She could hardly wallow in what was happening on the screen while the creator of it was standing so silently there.

'Enjoying it?' he asked.

'I *was*.'

'What did you think of Petronella?'

Tamsin sighed again. 'Why don't you sit down and watch it?'

'I never do.'

'You are now,' she pointed out.

'I was watching your reaction. It's interesting.'

'What is?' The commercial break came on, and she turned to look up at him. 'I'm just sitting here, not jumping up and down in excitement.' He perched himself on the arm of her chair and she moved uneasily. The man was impossible!

'True. But you haven't fallen asleep either. That's a good sign. I asked you what you thought of Petronella.'

'She's—a very interesting character.'

'Hmm. You don't recognise anything?'

She tore her eyes away from a scantily clad girl advertising lager, because anything was better than talking to him, and said: 'No. Why—should I?'

'She's a bit like you.'

'Well, you can hardly have based her on me, seeing that we hadn't met when you wrote it,' she answered smartly. '*And* I'm not sure if I find your comment at all flattering. She's——' she stopped.

'Yes? She's what?' he prompted.

'You should know, you made her up.'

'I'm interested. Pray tell. What is she?'

'She's a very determined and obstinate girl, and if I were Jason Ryder, I wouldn't put up——' she stopped again. The trap yawned open, and she had very nearly fallen right in it.

'You wouldn't put up with her nonsense? Just wait till act three and you'll find out whether he does or not. You've summed her up very neatly, Tammy. Thanks.' Blaise got up, as if to go.

'I'm *not* like her,' she said indignantly.

'No? Then just wait a few minutes. You'll see what I mean.' And he walked out.

Seething, Tamsin began to watch the second part. She wished he had never come in. She wished—but she wasn't sure what she wished any more, because she was drawn, unwillingly, into the story again. There was humour and drama in it, and what was more, she now found herself watching the main character, Petronella, with more than a passing interest. The plot of the play itself was deceptively simple: the conflict in a small village caused by a proposed motorway which might affect the life of the village itself—the main conflict being between Petronella Sims, the doctor's daughter, and Jason Ryder, lord of the manor and an aggressive handsome beast who thought the motorway would be a good thing. Petronella didn't, and was fighting tooth and nail to get it scrapped, cancelled or moved away. And now she and Jason were heading for another clash at a party to which both had been invited. Tamsin sat back and prepared for the fireworks. Blaise Torran had a nerve—but he also had a point. In some of Petronella's words she could almost hear herself...

'Ouch!' she winced out loud as the plate which Petronella had aimed at Jason went crashing into the wall and shattered, and Jason, white-faced, stalked towards her. They were in the kitchen of the house where the party was in progress, and were alone. Loud music and laughter and the clinking of glasses came from the other side of the door, but the atmosphere in the kitchen was anything but festive.

'Right,' said Jason, a very well known and popular actor, ideal for the part, and he smiled as he spoke. 'That's it. Miss High-and-Mighty Sims, you're going to get the spanking your father forgot to give you when you were younger. And I'm going to be the one to——'

'Like *hell* you are!' Petronella stood and defied him, arms akimbo, the perfect picture of affronted womanhood. 'You touch me and I'll——'

Tamsin covered her face with her hands and groaned. Oh dear, she knew quite suddenly exactly what Blaise had meant. She peeped through her fingers to see a glorious struggle going on, and just as it was getting interesting, the door burst open, and their shortsighted hostess came in.

'Dancing out here?' she trilled. 'What a lovely idea!' And the scene cut, leaving a brief glimpse of Jason's face before it did so. He looked as though he were going to burst out laughing.

The play went its inevitable course, alternately funny and sad and dramatic, with the beautifully satisfying ending where all was sorted out, the motorway diverted slightly away from the village to end up cutting right through Ryder Hall—which was precisely what Jason Ryder had been aiming towards all along, for the Hall, a magnificent mouldering old ruin, cost a fortune to run, without even touching the dry rot, woodworm and death watch beetle with which it was infested. The last brief scene showed Petronella and Jason, united at last, walking up the path towards a large pretty cottage outside which was a For Sale sign, and Jason uprooting the sign, dusting his hands, and saying: 'Let's go in. We've one or two things to discuss—like who's going to be boss.'

'Hmm.' Tamsin gave a pleased little sigh. Too many plays ended with a question mark, and the feeling that there should be another act, if only to explain. It made a pleasant change to see one neatly rounded off. She went out to make coffee, expecting to have to face subtle questioning. Blaise didn't even look up as she entered the kitchen, he was too engrossed in typing. To her enquiry as to whether he wanted coffee she got an abstracted grunt which she took to mean yes.

She made it, handed him his, and went out again. So much for worrying about how to answer him. He was probably not even aware she had been in the room. There seemed only one thing left to do—go to bed. She drank her coffee, switched off the television, and went.

When she got up at seven the following morning, the kettle was still faintly warm, as though Blaise had made coffee an hour or so previously. There were no papers out, and the typewriter was covered and standing on a cupboard in a corner, out of the way. Tamsin wondered how late he had stayed up. Four? Five? Anything was possible. It at least explained his inability to get up early. He was a night owl, wide awake at night, unwilling to surface until day was well begun. Tamsin smiled to herself at the thought. Then, her curiosity getting the better of her, she opened the cupboard beneath the typewriter. The paper was stacked neatly there, out of the way. She didn't intend to read any—or so she told herself—just to see how much he had written. And in the stack of typed paper there were at least forty pages. She glanced down the first page, that was all—but somehow it wasn't enough, and she read on to the second, and the third. Then, making herself a cup of tea, she sat down at the table and began to read the play properly. Because she couldn't help herself. She certainly couldn't have stopped, not then. After the first two pages, she was hooked.

The tea grew cold, forgotten, as she lost herself in the play—then a stair creaked, she heard movement, and guiltily she started to gather up the sheets. Too hastily—the tea went flying, and she watched in horror as the brown liquid spread its stain all over every page.

She snatched them up, and they dripped tea all over the table. She gazed at the door, waiting with dread for the footsteps, the accusing voice, the anger—but there was silence, and after a moment or two she began to breathe again. Very quietly she crept to the foot of the stairs and listened. Silence above. One of the children had obviously woken, gone to the bath-room, and was sound asleep again. And Tamsin was left with over forty pieces of neatly typed playscript, all of them, in some degree, bearing the stamp of her guilt. There was only one thing to do, and fast. She lifted the typewriter up and set it in a clean half of the table, cleared up the mess, stacked her paper beside her, and began to retype what she had ruined.

She was a fast worker, and well used to typing let-ters and reports, but a play was something completely different. She was tired after ten pages, and exhausted after twenty, and her eyes and fingers ached, and she realised, wryly, that it was a fitting punishment for her own curiosity. Taking a deep breath, she picked up page twenty-one, and started copying it out, word for word, line for line, space for space...

'And what the hell are you doing?'

She jumped, and the letters jumped, and she typed, 'zxcnm,.$\frac{1}{2}$' before looking up in dismay. 'Oh,' she said. 'Ah.'

'Oh, ah, indeed. But it doesn't tell me what you're playing at on my typewriter,' and he strode across, and picked up a handful of the browned paper. He didn't look remotely pleased. He looked, in fact, like a man who required an explanation. He glared down at her. 'Go on,' he said.

'I—I—I'm sorry,' she burst out.

'I should damn well think you are. But why is my work covered in this disgusting brown mess?'

'Tea,' she said helpfully, in a quiet murmur.

'I don't give it a damn what it is—it's ruined about nine hours of work!'

'I'm retyping it now——' she began.

'I didn't imagine you were sending letters to Father Christmas.' His tone wasn't exactly withering, it wasn't exactly caustic, and he didn't look as if he was prepared to believe any flights of fancy that flashed into Tamsin's mind on the lines of—I was passing the cupboard holding a cup of tea when the door flew open and I stumbled—so she swallowed, took a deep breath, and told the truth.

'You're bloody nosey,' he said. 'How would you like it if I read your diary?'

'It's not the same——' she began.

'Shut up! It's near enough. Serves you right anyway. I want that lot done fast. I like to read over what I've typed before I start writing again, so you can just get on with it.'

'That's what I was doing before you came sneaking down,' she answered hotly. She had had enough from this tall, arrogant, smouldering male, and her own temper rose to match his. If he thought he would lecture her he was mistaken! 'So shut up yourself and let me get on with it.' And she glared at him, her cheeks pink with anger. 'And if you want a cup of tea, make it yourself!' She banged the papers down, ripped the offending sheet out of the typewriter, and put in another one.

'Temper, temper,' he said softly, mockingly.

'Hah! You should talk! It's not as bad as yours, you aggressive beast!'

'But I don't go around spilling tea over other people's——'

'You're perfect!' she snapped. 'Your halo will

strangle you one of these days, and serve *you* right.'
She looked down at the paper beside her and began to
type. Unfortunately, his presence didn't help matters.
Her fingers found the wrong keys, she forgot the space
bar—and she knew, with dread certainty, that she
would have to do the page again. But not until he'd
gone. As long as she appeared to be typing well—only
then he came and stood just behind her, leaned over,
and began to read what she was typing.

'Good grief!' he said. 'Spare me. If that's the best
you can do you'd better not——' He got no further.
Tamsin jumped up, whirled round, and tried to push
him away.

'Go *away*!' she shouted. 'Just go away and leave
me——'

She shouldn't have tried to push him. She knew
that even as she did it. It was a foolish impulsive
action that she regretted instantly as she found herself
gripped and held, for she was powerless to move.

'Don't push me,' he said, ever so quietly, and all the
more menacingly for that, 'or you'll get the spanking
of your life——'

'You wouldn't dare,' she said through clenched
teeth. 'You *dare* to touch me——'

'Don't ever dare me,' he cut in. For a moment their
eyes met in a silent, powerful clash, and Tamsin,
determined she would not look away first, kept her
eyes steadily on his.

'I wouldn't—because you couldn't,' she answered
with scorn. 'You think you're Mr Universe, don't
you? Big deal! You're about as tough as——' but she
didn't get the chance to finish, because the next
moment he was in the chair, she was over his knee—
and she didn't know how it had happened.

'You were saying?'

'Ouch! Ah!' She kicked her feet wildly and he clamped his arm across them and stopped the flailing movement. 'Let me *go*—at *once*!'

'When you apologise for being such a quick-tempered little——'

'Go to hell!' She pummelled his leg with her arms, and then—Thwack! He smacked her soundly on her bottom, twice again, and then hauled her to her feet.

'Now, sit down, if you can, and get on with it. And the next time you feel like daring me to do anything, I suggest you hold your tongue.' He stood there, tall lean and powerful, and stared at Tamsin. She smarted, physically as well as mentally. But now her fight was gone. She knew now, with a stone cold certainty, that he meant every word he said. There was only one thing left for her to do: behave with dignity. She sat down at the table.

'I shall finish the typing,' she said. 'Just one thing. Your behaviour is quite despicable.' And she put in a fresh sheet of paper and began to type with great care.

'And yours is nearly impossible,' he replied, going over to the kettle. 'But you'll learn.'

She ignored his remark. She decided to ignore almost everything he said, unless the children were present. It could make life a lot easier. He made coffee for himself, and walked out, presumably to go back to bed. She didn't care where he went, as long as he was away from her. And she would make sure there were no mistakes in her work, so that he could not find fault.

The children came down shortly afterwards, and she put everything away carefully while she gave them breakfast. There would be no more accidents, especially not with marmalade and drinking chocolate around! They were filled with a lively curiosity as to why she should be working for Uncle Blaise, and Tamsin explained about the mishap, making light of it, and they accepted it with some amusement, then forgot immediately afterwards because they had more important things in mind, namely a game called Battleship which Blaise had shown them how to play the previous day, and which they intended to play together after breakfast.

Tamsin lit the fire for them and left them to it. All was peaceful once more. With any luck Blaise might stay asleep all morning. And she would find something to send him out for after lunch, if only bread, which was running short, due to the children's delight in feeding the birds with every scrap they could lay their hands on. She soon had the kitchen tidy, and set her work out again, and began typing. The peace didn't last long. The children started quarrelling, and Blaise came down, fully dressed and shaved, and clearly up for the day.

Tamsin looked at him as he came into the kitchen. Dignity, she reminded herself. Behave with dignity at all times. 'Do you want breakfast?' she asked him coolly.

'I'll get my own. You just carry on with your work.'

'Thank you, I intended to. However, I thought I would ask, as it is one of my tasks to do the cooking around here——'

'Spare me the sermon,' he pleaded. 'Toast doesn't require much culinary skill, I can manage that.'

Tamsin tightened her lips and continued with her typing. He was sarcastic, quite insufferable, and she must learn to ignore him. The only trouble with that was, he was a man who was impossible to ignore, a restless animal, vibrant with life and energy, he could no more be ignored than a tiger in the room. And he knew it. But Tamsin was going to try. It needed all her concentration, but she succeeded—for a few minutes. Blaise made his toast, buttered it, made coffee, stood leaning against the cupboard whistling quietly— and watching her. He was doing it deliberately, for reasons of his own, and Tamsin plodded on, her typing slower, but only fractionally, while she tried desperately to pretend he was just a piece of furniture, not *really* there, just something she didn't need to notice. It was no good. She made her second mistake on one line, knew she would make more if she carried on, so stopped and stood up, went over to the kettle, and made a cup of coffee. Then, because she didn't want to speak to him, and he had no intention of moving away, she went to the back door, opened it, and began scattering left-over crusts from breakfast to the waiting birds.

'We need some food,' she announced, without turning her back.

'Such as?'

'Cheese—butter—bread——'

'I'm not surprised, the amount you give those birds.'

'And milk,' she continued, as though he hadn't interrupted.

'Perhaps you could try them with bread and milk,' he suggested. 'I'm sure our feathered friends would like that. I'll just bring double the amount of milk back if you——'

'There will be no need, thank you.' She finished her task, dusted the crumbs from her hands and came

back into the kitchen. 'I'll make you a list now. Will
you go before lunch, or after?'

'When would you prefer?' he asked, as if willing to
co-operate in anything she suggested. Tamsin bit back
the natural retort which sprang to her lips, remembering that it would most definitely not be dignified if she
told him that as far as she was concerned he could go
just as soon as possible and stay away for hours and
hours.

She smiled instead. It was getting a little easier. 'It's
immaterial to me. I merely wished to know so that I
could prepare lunch in good time.'

'Then I'll go now. Make your list. I'll see if the kids
want to go.'

She sat down and wrote out a very neat and precise
list of food while he went out. She heard him talking
to the children, their voices coming in faintly from the
lounge, heard their laughter in response. They were
obviously going to go. Good. With nothing to distract
her, she would be able to get on much faster.

They all returned, wearing warm anoraks, the children clearly excited at the prospect of a ride with their
uncle. Tamsin handed him the list, and watched his
eyes skim down it.

One eyebrow rose slowly. 'Bubble bath?' he re-
marked. '*That's* food?'

'I'll pay you for that,' she responded calmly.
'There's none here, and I——'

'Doesn't matter, I'll get some. Sure I can't get you
anything else? Make-up?'

'I rarely wear any.' She smiled kindly. The conversation was all sweetness and light—on the surface.

'No,' he said dryly, 'I had noticed.' Tamsin turned

away before she said something she might regret.

'A drink of milk before you go, children?' she asked.

'No, thanks,' they chorussed.

'Okay, we're off. All right if we go in your car? The keys are in the hall.'

'Of course. If it needs petrol, I'll pay you when you return.'

'I'll see. Say goodbye to Tammy, kids.' And he walked out.

''Bye, Tammy.' They scampered after him. She heard the door slam, and sat down slowly. She was alone in the house for the first time since her arrival, and it suddenly seemed very quiet and empty. She corrected her mistakes, and continued her typing at a brisk pace. Soon she would prepare the lunch. She had managed to put the morning's humiliating incident out of her mind almost completely. Almost ...

It was nearly three o'clock when they returned, which annoyed Tamsin considerably, despite the fact that she had managed in the time to nearly complete the typing she had to do. It was, she told herself as she heard the front door knocker, typical man-like behaviour to stay out for hours, when, for all he knew, lunch could have been ruined.

They marched in, children first, carrying bulging plastic bags, followed by Blaise. She looked pointedly at her watch, and he said: 'Yes, I know we're late.'

'You are somewhat,' she agreed. There would be no scenes—not while they had company. 'Fortunately I've done a casserole. I'll clear the table and you can sit down. Go up and wash your hands, children.'

They ran out, giggling and laughing, and Tamsin

took all her work off the table. She couldn't resist it. 'If you'd any manners you'd have phoned to say you'd be ages,' she said in icy tones. 'How was I to know——'

'And if you'd any sense you'd have seen that your spare tyre was at least inflated,' he cut in. 'Because we had a puncture, didn't we? And don't try talking to me like a wife, I can do without nagging women——'

'A wife!' she burst out. 'No woman with any sense would marry *you*!' She glared at him, forgetting her mental vows of behaving in a dignified manner at all times.

'Well, you certainly wouldn't,' he agreed calmly— which only infuriated her more. '*You're* a man-hater, aren't you?' And he smiled in a certain way.

Tamsin whirled away, banging the typewriter down. She kept hold of it after she had put it on the cupboard top, hands gripping it tightly. He couldn't know what his words had done to her. An image of Nigel rose, and she felt almost sick. Without another word she walked out of the room and ran up the stairs, into her bedroom. She could hear the children talking, and taps running in the bathroom as she stood just inside her room holding the door, trying desperately to regain self-control. She breathed deeply and slowly. The mental picture of Nigel was already fading. In another minute she would be all right. She had to be...

She opened the door. 'Come along, children,' she called. 'Lunch is ready. I'm sure your hands are clean now.'

Paula came out first. 'We had a lovely ride with Uncle,' she said, as they went down the stairs to- gether. 'He took us in a café for lemonade and then we got a puncture——' she giggled.

'And he swore when he tried to put the spare tyre on,' said Peter, relishing the memory. ''Cos we had to drive *very slowly* to a garage to get it blown up. And he got the other tyre mended.'

'Did he?' Tamsin's heart sank. 'I must thank him.' She didn't want to see the look on his face when she did. She didn't want to talk to him either, but there was no choice. His words, those hurtful words, echoed in her ears. Said without apparent thought—or had they been? She couldn't be sure, which made it, in a way, worse. He knew exactly what he was doing all the time. And if he had said them with the object of hurting her unbearably, he had succeeded.

As they walked into the kitchen, Tamsin mentally braced herself. She need not have bothered. Blaise was skimming through what she had typed, and he looked up as they went in, and nodded. 'Not bad,' he said. Perhaps he was capable of switching his mind from one subject to another. There was certainly none of the mockery she had expected to see. 'You're nearly finished?'

'Yes. Another hour and I'll be done.' She busied herself with plates and cutlery. 'Thank you for getting the tyre mended. If you'll let me know how much——'

'Forget it.'

'But I——'

'Sit down, children.' He walked over to her at the cooker. 'I'm using your car, I'll pay for petrol and any other expenses while I do so.' The level brown eyes were hard and steady on her.

'Very well.' She handed him two plates. 'Those are the children's.'

She felt stifled, and that was unnerving. Before, if the two children had been present, the atmosphere was almost normal. But now, subtly, everything had changed. She was no longer as sure of herself as she had been. And he knew—that was the worst thing. But there was no running away. She was here, doing a job, and would be for at least a week longer. It seemed an endless stretch of time. She had to sit down and eat, but she didn't feel hungry, not at all.

CHAPTER SIX

THE children were in bed; all was quiet. Blaise was in the kitchen—presumably working, although Tamsin hadn't bothered to find out. She had managed fairly successfully to keep out of his way since lunch, and intended to keep on doing so as long as possible. She was reading when he came in, and her heart stopped for a moment, then began to pound. Nothing showed. She stared resolutely at the page in front of her, taking nothing in, apparently engrossed.

'Busy?' She couldn't be sure if there was any mockery in that brief word. She looked up.

'I'm reading. Why? Do you want something?'

'I'm not writing tonight. Not yet anyway. I thought we might talk about your work at the agency—unless, of course, the book is too absorbing to leave.'

'Well, I certainly couldn't read it with you hovering round.' She snapped it shut. 'What do you want to know?'

'Anything and everything. The day-to-day running of the place for a start, I suppose. I'll leave it to you.'

Tamsin looked at him with barely concealed dislike. He just didn't care about anything except himself. He stood there tall and arrogant, looking down at her as if he expected co-operation with his whims. And she was sure, without a doubt, that he'd have forgotten completely how he had hurt her. Twice—mentally, and physically.

She took a deep breath. 'All right. Don't you want to make notes?'

'I've a tape recorder—if you don't object to me using it.'

'Object? Would it make any difference if I did?' she answered, astonished.

His answer surprised her. 'Yes. I wouldn't use it if you said no, I'd make notes instead. It happens to be easier, that's all.' And, in spite of herself, she felt as though she had been childish.

'You'd better get it. I don't mind.'

Blaise went out, and Tamsin rubbed her burning forehead. She wished he didn't have the effect he did on her. He made her feel confused—and she didn't like it.

'Okay.' He had come silently back, carrying a small black portable cassette recorder. 'I'll put more coal on and make us a drink before we start. Tea or coffee?'

'Er—coffee, please.' She was alone again. She heard the tap running, the kettle going on, heard him whistling softly, the clatter of cups, and she had a sudden pang of awareness, a bittersweet awareness of loss, of what was gone for ever. Yet she could not explain it. She began to compose herself mentally for the ordeal which lay ahead. Normally she would have enjoyed it, with anyone else, but not with him, not him.

Yet, some time later, and to her own inward astonishment, she found herself doing just that. All thoughts of boring him stiff with the dullest cases she could think of had gone. For he was, in a way, like a skilful interviewer, and his manner was so completely different from what it had ever been that it had disarmed her.

Her mind was stimulated by his questions, by the gentle incisive probing into her memory, and she found herself recalling far more than she had ever realised she could. They all poured out; the funny, the tragic, the human drama, the whole kaleidoscope of glorious colour that made up a complete picture of her life and work with her father.

'... and then the son turned up from Australia. The solicitors working with us on the case had warned us he might, and that he was a trouble-maker, and they were right.' She paused as Blaise held up his hand to silence her.

'Hold it. I'll have to change the tape over.'

Tamsin was only mildly surprised. 'Doesn't it last long?'

'An hour each side,' was the dry answer. She looked at the clock, disbelieving her eyes.

'I've been talking into that for *an hour*?'

'You have. Want a rest—and a drink before we begin again?'

Her throat was dry, now that he mentioned it. She nodded. 'I think I will.'

'I've got some wine in my car. Do you drink?'

'Sometimes. Wine will do nicely.'

He vanished, she heard the front door open, and then silence for a few minutes, the door was firmly closed, and he came in carrying two bottles, white and red. 'I'll get the glasses,' he said. 'Keep in your mind what you're going to say next—though I've a good idea what's going to happen.'

'You'd never guess in a million years,' she said, amused.

'Wouldn't I? We'll see.' He went out, to return

with two glasses which he put down on the table next to the cassette.

'All right, what's your idea?' she asked, watching him pour out the white wine she had indicated.

'That the son hoped for half the old lady's possessions, and with there being no will——' he paused, passed her a glass, and lifted an enquiring eyebrow.

'Right so far. Go on.' She sipped the cool sweet wine. It went down like nectar.

'Legally, her house and possessions would go jointly to him and the unmarried daughter who's stayed at home to look after her all those years—and I'll bet you didn't like that, nor the solicitors, nor the daughter. Right?'

She nodded. 'Would you?'

'No. I didn't like the sound of him when you started the story. But my guess is, you found the will, and he didn't get a bean.'

She stared at him, dismayed. 'Aren't you the clever one!'

'I'm a writer. My imagination works on the lines of the improbable. But I'd still like to hear it in your own words.' He pressed the 'record' button.

'Well, as I told you, we'd been hired originally to provide a sort of bodyguard-cum-escort for old Mrs Brewer——' she stopped, alarmed. 'Oh! I said her name—I didn't mean——' He stopped the tape.

'Do you want me to erase that bit and start again? You have my word that anything on the tape is heard only by me, no one else, ever. I wipe them out when I've got all the ideas I want.'

She shook her head. 'As long as you give your word.' She indicated he could start it, and he did so.

'She was a bit of an old dragon, really, yet terribly afraid of being robbed—she must have led her daughter a heck of a life. Margaret—the daughter—was one of those pale, shadowy creatures who was completely dominated by her mother. We all felt terribly sorry for her, but there was nothing we could do, and when old Mrs Brewer died we assumed that Margaret would naturally inherit everything—which was no more than she deserved—and when she came to us a week or so later to say that it seemed there was no will, and could we help, because her brother in Australia was coming home—after thirty years, incidentally, of never even bothering to write or phone or even send Christmas cards—we had to do something.' She paused. She was going to enjoy the next bit. Even though Blaise had guessed, he couldn't imagine the reality.

'With Margaret's help, we took the house apart—metaphorically speaking—and it was some task, believe me. The place was crammed with paintings, ornaments, huge Victorian furniture, stuffed birds in glass cases—you name it, it was there. But there was no sign of any will. And the son was staying in the best hotel in the village, and calling on his sister every day, making her more nervous than ever.' She paused and drank some wine. 'I met him, when I was at the house, going through a trunkful of old papers. A big, swaggering man of about fifty-five, a few years older than Margaret, wealthy—or so he said and acted—and totally uncaring of everything she had done. He just wanted his share, and intended getting it. But worse than that, his plan was to sell the house so that he could have half the money from it, and then just go back to Australia. She didn't have the money to buy half from him.' Unknowingly, Tamsin clenched her

fists at the memory of the man whose insolent manner
and even more insolent eyes had filled her with loath-
ing.

'It seemed there was nothing we could do except let
events take their natural course. And then, one
day——' she paused deliberately and a slow smile came
over her face, and she picked up her glass and sipped
reflectively. Blaise jabbed the 'off' button.

'So help me—I could strangle you,' he said, and
Tamsin looked at him in amazement, lost in the enjoy-
ment of the wine, and the satisfying memories.

'What?' she gasped. 'What do——'

'For God's sake, get to the point!' he exclaimed.
'Dammit, I'm sitting on the edge of my chair in sus-
pense and you drift off into a daydream!'

Tamsin began to laugh. He wasn't joking, which
perversely made it even more amusing. 'I'm sorry.'
She sobered. 'But what happened next was so—
almost poetic, in a way—and to see his face when we
told him. Ah!' she gave a satisfied sigh.

'Will—you—get—on—with—it?' said Blaise omin-
ously slowly, and Tamsin gave a brisk nod.

'Of course.' She cleared her throat. 'Picture the
scene. I'd finished going through the papers—it took
three days—and I was sitting having a cup of coffee
with Margaret when her brother strode in. I saw her
face tighten and change. She almost cringed—I hated
him, believe me. He began lecturing her about the
state of the garden shed and how she'd let it go and it
was a pity he'd not been there to keep an eye on things
and she'd had a cushy life—and so on, and I could
have cheerfully hit him on the head with the vase by
my chair—when something clicked in my brain. We'd
gone through the house with a fine tooth comb, but

we'd never even dreamed of looking at the garden shed because as far as we knew the old lady never went out there, only to sit just outside the lounge in her chair on fine days. But something else clicked at the same time. Just before old Mrs Brewer had died, and Margaret had been by her side then, as always, she had clutched her hand and said: "Will the flowers." We'd thought it was the *beginning* of a sentence—but then suddenly I saw it in a new light. What she might have been trying to say—and been too ill to do—could have been—"the will is near the flowers." I couldn't wait until the brother had gone, and I went outside to the garden shed, which was full of plant pots, tools, packets of seeds from the year dot, etcetera—and I began looking. I was filthy after five minutes——' She stopped.

'But you found it?' he asked, as if, for once, he couldn't help himself.

She smiled, a beautiful dreamy smile. 'Oh yes, I did—thanks to that horrible man. It was there, in a large dusty old envelope at the back of a shelf piled high with catalogues for plants and flowers. And that was that. Because the old lady left everything to Margaret. The will had been made fifteen years previously, when Mrs Brewer was active enough to have hidden it, and she'd had a different solicitor then, in another town, which was why the present one knew nothing. But two very satisfying things came out of it all. One—I timed my moment carefully, and told the son precisely *how* I'd got the idea of looking in the garden shed—and he went a very strange colour. You know, for a moment I actually thought he was going to have a heart attack—or hit me—only luckily for me, my father was in the room at the time. The son just walked out, and I never saw him again.'

'And the other satisfying event?'

'Ah yes,' she sighed. 'That was even better. But it didn't concern the work directly, so——' she paused.

'But you're going to tell me?'

'If you like. It was Margaret. She now had sufficient money, and a glorious old house stuffed with valuable antiques, to live comfortably for the rest of her life. But she had had no life, not really, and she was shy and timid and unsure of herself.' She stopped, remembering her difficulty in persuading the woman.

'And?' Blaise asked impatiently. She looked at him. Where was the aggressive man she knew and disliked? He sat there, and he looked almost human—almost concerned.

'Can't you guess?'

'I can—but I'd like you to tell me.'

'All right, I will. I managed to persuade her to let me take her into Manchester, to the top hairdressers. I had to go with her and virtually hold her hand all the way. She had the long mousy mane she'd always worn in a bun cut and shaped and streaked with gold—and wow! the transformation!' She laughed. 'I couldn't believe my eyes, but more to the point, neither could she! The rest was easy. New clothes—a whole outfit of mix and match suits, trousers, sweaters, the lot, and then we went to see a beautician who made her up and showed her how to make herself up—and you know, she suddenly emerged into a darned attractive woman. But she was still shy, underneath it all. She kept asking me—how can it last? I'm just me. So I took her into one of those model agencies——' she stopped at his disbelieving exclamation, and looked at him.

'You didn't! What the hell for?'

She gave him a very superior smile. There were, apparently, things that even he didn't know. It made her feel quite good. 'Not to be a model! Did you think that?' she laughed. 'They run courses for house-wives, secretaries—anyone who can pay, and wants that bit of know-how. They teach you how to walk, how to sit and stand gracefully, in short, how to be more poised. If you're overweight they tell you what to eat and what not to eat. Margaret was slim—too slim—so they showed her how to put *on* a few pounds. And at the end of three months,' she sighed gently, 'I helped her give her first party. No one would have recognised her. She was, quite simply, a new woman. We still see each other every few weeks, and she's leading a pleasantly busy social life, and doing voluntary work in the local hospital—and if ever Dad's secretary's off, she insists on coming in to do the typing and so on. That was one of our more successful cases, you could say.'

'You should be a writer,' Blaise said suddenly.

'What?' Tamsin stared at him. 'Are you trying to be funny?'

'Do I look as though I am?' He looked, in fact, quite serious.

She shook her head. He switched off the tape recorder. 'We'll have a break.' Then, quite suddenly, Tamsin began to feel uncomfortable. While they had been doing the tape, it had been all right, quite impersonal, and that way was easier. But she wasn't used to him being human—only with the children—and she felt, absurdly, as if she couldn't cope.

She began to rise from her chair. 'I'll go and look at the children,' she said.

'No, I'll go. You stay there.' And he went. Tamsin

moved uneasily. What was it in his manner? She didn't know, only that, for the past hour or so, she had found herself relaxing in his company, almost off guard, and it was disturbing.

'They're okay, fast asleep.' He was back, and stood there by the fire.

'I can't think of any more cases tonight,' she blurted out. 'Can we leave it till another time?'

'Sure.' He shrugged. 'I appreciate all the material you've given me.'

'There's a film I want to watch,' she said.

'Then I'll go and make notes from these tapes.' He picked up the cassette recorder, and started to walk towards the door. As he reached it, and began to pull it open, he half turned towards her. She sensed something, but had no idea what, and his words had the greater effect for that. 'By the way,' he said, 'who's Nigel?'

The question hit her with the force of a blow, and she felt the blood drain from her face. She stared at him, numbed and shocked. 'How did you know?' she whispered.

He closed the door and came back across the room towards her. 'I don't know anything,' he said, 'except that you were moaning his name in your sleep last night, and I——'

'Please go away,' she said. Her lips felt frozen, as though she could hardly get the words out. This, on top of everything else that had happened in one day, was too much. She managed to stand up. 'I don't want to talk about——'

'He's the man, isn't he?' he asked softly. He was watching her, just looking at her, and no expression in his eyes save that hard coolness she now knew so well.

She drew in her breath sharply. If she didn't get out, away from him——

'You know nothing,' she gasped. 'Nothing! I'm going——'

He caught her arm. 'Wait——'

'No. Let me *go*!' She swung away from him and made for the door. She expected any second that he would go after her, but he didn't. She grabbed her car keys from the hall table and opened the front door. An icy blast of air swept in, making her shiver, but she went out, slamming the door behind her, and ran to her car. If she could get away for a while, just to think—that was all. Just to get away from him and his cold eyes and probing scalpel of questions. She was in the car now, key in ignition, and then——

Blaise reached in, took out the keys, and said: 'Don't be stupid. You're coming in.'

'I'm going for a drive. Do you mind?' She tried to snatch her keys back, but he held them out of reach.

'You're not going anywhere. Now, are you coming in under your own steam or do I carry you?'

'I'm staying here until you give me——' She didn't have time to finish the sentence. He reached in, lifted her bodily out of the seat, and carried her into the house, slamming both car door and front door closed with his foot. He carried her, struggling and swearing, to the kitchen, dumped her down by the table, and said:

'I did that for your own good. I couldn't leave the kids alone and go searching for you if you landed upside down in a ditch, could I?'

Her answer was brief, silent and eloquent. She swung her arm round at him, and if the blow had connected he would have rocked on his feet. But it didn't. He caught her arm and held it. 'Don't try and fight me,' he began. 'You can't——'

'Then leave me *alone*,' she gasped. 'What are you? D-do you enjoy seeing p-people suffer?'

'No. I asked a question because I wanted to know. And now I do.'

'You don't,' she said fiercely. 'You can only guess. Well, guess what you like, I don't care,' but she stopped, because her voice was wobbling, and she ached all over, and slowly, he released her.

'I'll make you a cup of tea.'

'I don't want a cup of tea from you. I'll make my own.' She turned away from him and went over to the sink. Then he was behind her, moving silently.

'Tammy,' he said, 'I'm sorry. I wouldn't have asked you if I'd known it would hurt you——'

'Of course you would!' she whirled round to face him. 'That's how you get your kicks. Well, here's another one for you. I fell in love when I was nineteen, with a man who was so wonderful in every way that I knew all I wanted to do was spend the rest of my life with him,' she paused, and the tears glinted in her eyes, making the room, and him, blurred and almost unreal. 'So you can have a good laugh about that. Go on!' He stood silent, unmoving.

'Not funny so far? Then I'll tell you the rest. I went out with him for six months, and life was marvellous, and we planned a holiday abroad, and everything was booked, and I was about to leave for the airport to meet him there—my father was just getting the car out—when there was a ring at the door, and a woman stood there. A nice, pleasant little woman who said she had something to tell me rather urgently. So I said I was in a hurry, because I was just going on holiday and she said, yes, that was why she had come, and I'd better listen, and then decide whether I still wanted to go——'

She stopped there, because the memories she had suppressed for so long—too long—the memories of that unbearable, humiliating final scene came rushing back so forcefully that it was as if it were all happening again. The woman's face, her words, the words she had held back for too long and which now, undamned, came pouring out in a rush, until, shocked and white-faced, Tamsin had taken her into the house, and they had talked for nearly an hour, while her father, ever tactful, had gone off to make them tea, and leave them alone, and put the car away, because by then he had heard enough to know that Tamsin would not be going on holiday with Nigel.

The woman was his wife, and she had only found out by accident of Tamsin's existence that morning when she had discovered a letter from her, which made it only too clear that Tamsin thought Nigel was single. And she had seen Tamsin's photo with the letter, and known she wasn't just another woman.

'... for I wasn't the first, not by a long shot. That was what made it, if possible, even worse. But the worst thing of all was that he had two children. She—she showed me their photographs.' Tamsin closed her eyes, and because she did, she was not aware of the expression on Blaise's face.

She went on, because it was too late to stop now, and because she could no longer help herself: 'A nasty little story. But one that happens all over the world, all the time—only knowing that doesn't take away the pain, does it? It doesn't make you stop loving someone either—and I still hurt—and——' she stopped. 'I'm going to bed. Don't worry, you can keep the keys—I shan't be trying to run away again. You can't run away from yourself, I realise that now.' She had opened her eyes, and she couldn't meet his, for fear of what she might see there. She turned away and walked out of the kitchen, away from him and his pity—or perhaps from his scorn. She didn't know which, and she didn't want to find out. Slowly, feeling as if she was terribly heavy, and every movement was an effort, she went up the stairs, and to bed.

When she awoke in the morning, it was as if a burden had been lifted from her. She sat up in bed and looked around the room, and she thought, in wonder: I'm cured. There was no dull ache any more, no reluctance to think of his name. It was as if he had never existed. She had slept deeply and soundly, the sleep of utter mental exhaustion. She stretched her arms, and then shivered. The room was cold, and the light was bright from outside. Pulling on a dressing gown, Tamsin went to the window and flung back the curtains to a scene of Christmas card whiteness. During the night it had snowed, and everything was covered in a soft white blanket, only the trees sharply etched in black making a stark contrast. She gazed out in contentment, gave a little sigh, then went downstairs to make herself a cup of tea.

It was not yet seven, but she was wide awake, and filled with a kind of calmness that she accepted, even though she didn't fully understand it. It was enough, for the moment. She began to make her breakfast, of tea and toast. She had several jobs to do, and the sooner the better, then there would be plenty of time to play with the children, perhaps even build a snowman in the garden.

She turned on the radio and listened to the music while she ate her toast and sat warming herself by the fire. There were papers on the table, and the tape recorder, but she didn't feel concerned about what Blaise had been doing. She felt instead a curiously empty sensation when she thought of him, and she shivered slightly. She thought she knew why. She had exorcised the ghosts of the past, but he had been instrumental in making her do so, and because of that, she felt as though she wanted nothing more to do with him. It was impossible, because he was there, and would be for as long as she stayed, and the children's welfare was the most important thing—but she thought that if it could be possible not to have to speak to him at all, not to have to look at him, or be near him, she would be satisfied.

It was as if all her dislike of him had concentrated and become almost overwhelming. Surely he wouldn't speak to her again about Nigel? But nothing was certain about Blaise. If he tried to, she would just walk away—it was the only thing to do. And yet he could be frightening at times. He had lifted her out of the car and carried her back in the house as if she were a child—and then he had made her tell him. She couldn't even remember now exactly how it had come about. The scene was a confused blur. Only the image of Blaise remained, inexorable, powerful, and waiting. Waiting for her to tell him—and she had.

She put her hand to her mouth. He frightens me, she thought. It's as if he sees everything differently from other people. As if he can see into my mind, and

I don't like it. I didn't before, but I like it even less now, after what happened. She looked at the papers on the table, and for the first time she wondered if he had written anything down about what she had told him of Nigel.

Standing up, careful to put her tea cup on the sink first, she went to the table and began to read the papers. There were notes about the taped interview, and that was all. The story of Margaret and the search for the missing will was written down in more detail than the other cases, as if it had interested him more, but that was all. There was nothing about Tamsin herself. She looked up and out of the window. She hadn't really expected he would, had she? On a sudden impulse, she switched on the recorder and put it to rewind, then went and turned off the radio. She wondered how everything sounded now—and a lot of the things she told him had been quite off the cuff, due to his expert questioning, brought out from the recesses of her mind, and forgotten almost immediately afterwards. It whirred, then clicked to a stop, and she pressed the arrow to run it from the beginning of side two.

Her voice came out loudly and clearly. 'Well, as I told you, we'd been hired originally to provide a sort of bodyguard-cum-escort for old Mrs Brewer—oh! I said her name—I didn't mean——' There was a click, a brief silence before the tape continued, and she remembered that Blaise had stopped it because of her alarm over the name. She listened, fascinated at hearing her own words telling the story, and washed her plate and cup while it went on, and on, until it reached the final bit. '... you should be a writer.' His deep voice came over very clearly, as did her reply.

'What? Are you trying to be funny?' 'Do I look as though I am?'

Then it clicked off, and as Tamsin dried her hands preparatory to switching off the cassette there was a further click and she heard, even as her finger reached out to press the 'stop' button—'No. Let me *go*!' Then footsteps, a door slamming, some blurred sounds, a bang, then silence. But she stood there, eyes wide and horrified. Because that had been *her* voice—and what was it doing on the tape? Then she heard again, movements, footsteps, and then his voice, very close and clear: 'I did that for your own good. I couldn't leave the kids alone and go searching for you if you landed upside down in a ditch, could I?'

And she realised exactly what she was listening to. As every word came over, loud and clear, of that brief, unforgettable painful scene in the kitchen the previous night, she relived every moment in a kind of agonised horror. He hadn't made notes because he hadn't needed to. He had taped it instead. He had cold-bloodedly recorded every word, and for what reason? There was only one thing she could think of: so that he could use that too in one of his plays.

She listened numbly right up till the last words, and then there was silence, only the whirring of the tape until at last, minutes later, it clicked to a stop. Tamsin had never in her life been filled with such an over-whelming hurt and anger. It was a dangerous combination. She felt icy cold. If she could have killed Blaise at that moment she thought she might have done so. But he wasn't there; he was in bed. Taking a deep breath, she picked up the recorder and walked along the hall, up the stairs. Her brain was functioning almost mechanically, which enabled her to close quietly the door of the children's room before opening his. Then she closed his door very softly and walked over to the bed where he lay fast asleep.

For a few moments she watched him, filled with hatred so overwhelming that she could scarcely breathe. There was a glass of water on his bedside table. She put down the tape recorder, picked up the glass, and emptied it over his face. Then she hit him as hard as she could. Not once, but twice, three times—until he sat up, gasping, saw her, grabbed hold of her with a force she had never before known, flung her across the bed, and pinioned her down beside him.

CHAPTER SEVEN

'You bitch!' he said harshly. 'You absolute little——'

Panting, gasping for breath, Tamsin glared up at him. 'I could kill you,' she whispered. 'I wish I was a man so I could break every bone—you are despicable!' She struggled violently to free herself, but he only gripped her the more fiercely, holding her down so firmly that it hurt her to move. 'Let me go or I'll scream!'

'Will you? See if you like this, then.' He moved so swiftly she could not guess his intent, and clamped his hand over her mouth. 'Now try.'

She tried to bite his hand, but couldn't. He went on: 'You're mad. You think I'm going to lie there while you attack me? My God, you deserve a darned good hiding—but I'm going to give you one chance. Just one. You'll tell me now why you came raging up, and I'll listen, but I warn you, it had better be good, because one thing's sure, I don't like being woken up by having water thrown at me. I'm going to take my hand from your mouth, and you can speak. Don't try and scream, because if you do, you'll be sorry. Do I make myself clear? I'm not joking. I'm about ready to forget you're a woman and give you a damn good beating!' He took his hand away.

'You know why,' she gasped. 'I played *the tape*.' She was nearly crying with white-hot temper.

'What the hell does that mean?'

'Don't pretend. Don't lie. That makes it worse. You recorded *every word*. You are loathsome. I hate you so much I could——' she stopped to take breath, and hear him say:

'I don't know what you're talking about.'

'Yes, you do!' she said fiercely. 'It's all there—I brought it up——'

'Hold it!' He sat up and released her, then looked at the tape recorder on his bedside table. 'That—you brought that up. Why?'

'I just told you—I heard it all, every word. I p-played it while I was eating breakfast.'

'So?'

Tamsin put her head in her hands. He just didn't care—that made it so much worse that she felt sick. He didn't even think he'd done anything wrong. She wanted to scream.

Then his voice came, quieter, less violent. 'Look, I think we've got a crossed line somewhere. You knew I was taping everything you said. You agreed——'

'Not *that*. Not what I told you about Nigel—oh, how could you!'

'*What?* What the hell are you saying?'

She didn't answer. Instead she leaned over, pressed the rewind button for a few moments, then started it going. It began in the middle, and when she saw by his face that he had heard enough, she stopped it. '*That's* what I'm saying,' she said, trembling.

'My God!' Blaise looked as shocked as she had, when she had first heard the tape herself. Without another word Tamsin got up and walked out of the room, down the stairs, into the kitchen where she collapsed into a chair and the tears came at last, not burning tears of shame and betrayal. She heard nothing, yet a few moments later he spoke from beside her.

'I swear to you I know nothing about it,' he said.

She looked up unseeing, blinded by tears. 'How can you say that?' she said shakily. 'You don't even care, do you?'

He pulled up a chair. 'Tamsin, listen to me. Listen very carefully. I don't know what kind of man you think I am, but I swear to you on my honour that I would never record a private conversation—which is what that was, last night.'

She sniffed. 'Then how did it get on it?'

'I don't know. But I'll find out. Think—think carefully, and try to remember what happened. When we were in the lounge I was about to carry the recorder out to the kitchen—we'd finished our interview, remember?' She nodded. 'Then I asked who Nigel was. Right?'

'Yes,' she whispered. 'Wait—hadn't we better rewind to where it starts, then——' her voice trailed away.

'If you can bear it.'

'Yes.' She found the button. 'I'll do it. I've a rough idea where.' She found it, then it began. And somehow, now, it wasn't quite as bad, because she sensed he spoke the truth.

'No, let me *go*!' she heard, for the second time. Blaise reached out and stopped it.

'That was when we were standing in the lounge and I'd caught your arm and said "wait" and you'd turned away—but I was still holding the recorder—and then you dashed out of the room, remember?'

'Yes.'

'Tamsin, I think you could have knocked it on

then. Let's listen some more.' He started it up, and speaking quietly, said: 'As you dashed out of the front door I took this into the kitchen and put it on the table, but it was recording as I set it down—that would be the bang—and I never noticed. I wanted to get after you.' He stopped. 'And if it was, as I'm beginning to think now, it would go on recording so that when we came back in——' he stopped as on the tape they heard clearly the words and movement as they had their stormy conversation—and somehow it all fitted in. He switched it off. 'I think we've heard enough.'

'B-but when you played it back to make notes, why didn't you hear it?' she said shakily.

'Because the minute we'd finished talking about Margaret, I switched off. Why should I keep it on? If I had, I would have heard what you heard and erased it—then you wouldn't have come tearing up to rend me limb from limb.'

It all had such a ring of truth that there seemed only one thing left to say. 'I'm sorry I attacked you,' she said.

He stood up. 'Forget it. I'm going up to get changed. I'll be down in ten minutes.' Tamsin watched him go. She watched him, and the calmness was shattered beyond repair. She felt emotionally drained, empty. She felt as if she had lived through a lifetime in the past thirty minutes—and in a strange way, it was as though nothing would ever be the same again. There was no explaining it, yet something had changed, and she with it. And when Blaise came down a short time later, she knew what it was.

She was making toast when he came into the room, and she turned to tell him, and it was as if it was all happening in slow motion—as if she had time to see everything clearly—and to know. She saw him, she saw the casual grey sweater and jeans he wore, she saw the size of him, and his face, freshly washed and shaved, with a scratch down one cheek either where he had cut himself, or she had caught him with her hand—and in that instant of awareness she knew why she had disliked him so from the first instant of seeing —she knew why he so frightened her, and she knew why every sense in her body had warned her he was dangerous.

The grill pan clattered to the floor, scattering half-toasted bread as she jerked away hastily, her hand knocking it out. 'Oh, hell!'

'Leave it, I'll pick it up.' Could he know? He gave her an odd look as he bent to pick up the pieces. 'No damage done.' He brushed the toast on his sleeve. 'Good as new. Is it for me?'

'Yes, but I'll——'

'Do more? No, you won't. Sit down. Want a cup of tea?'

'Please.' She sat down obediently, because it was easier not to have to think at that moment.

'Did you say you'd eaten?' he asked.

'Yes. It's been snowing.' It was a stupid thing to say, considering the weather hadn't been mentioned, and she felt herself go pink. He appeared not to notice the absurdity.

'So I see. The kids will like it.'

'Yes.'

'Sure you're not hungry?'

'I couldn't eat a thing.' That was the truth, anyway. And what do I do now? she thought. It's ridiculous to feel like this about a man like him, and it hurts like hell and I don't think I can bear it. 'Sorry?'

'I said, do you feel all right? You're as white as a sheet.'

'I don't know.' She closed her eyes, but the room started going round, so she opened them again.

'You'd better go back to bed. I'll see to the children when they wake.'

'But I'll be——' Tamsin began.

'Do as you're told. I'll bring your tea up.'

Without a word she went, lay down, covered herself up and waited. Blaise came in very quietly a few minutes later and handed her a beaker. 'Want an aspirin or anything?'

'No, thanks.' She didn't want to look at him, but she did, and it hurt. He sat down on the bed, not too near.

'Tamsin?'

'Yes?'

'What is it? I've erased the tape. It's gone for good.'

'Oh, I don't know——' she burst into tears, hating herself, hating him, and the whole world. She fumbled for the handkerchief she kept under her pillow and he found it for her and gave it to her. 'I'll be fine in a minute,' she lied desperately. If only he would *go*! Her humiliation was bad enough without him seeing. Through choking sobs she went on: 'I've got a headache, that's all.'

'Does it make you cry?'

'Yes—no—oh! please go away.'

He stood up. 'All right, stay in bed. I'll look in later.' And he went out. Alone, Tamsin sat up and drank the tea. Then she lay down, and thought about the impossible situation she found herself in. She didn't like him, so how could she love him? But she did. One thing was certain: he must never know. The next week or so would soon pass, and then it would be goodbye. And that would be that. She'd get over it— soon. At least he'd cured her of Nigel. She closed her eyes, and soon she dozed off.

She was half awake when she heard the door creak, and she closed her eyes, breathing deeply and evenly. She was aware of him in the room, but he didn't speak. She was very conscious of him watching her, and it took all her self-control to keep her breathing steady. Then soft footsteps, the door creaked, and silence. She opened her eyes—and Blaise was standing just inside the door. Her heart leapt with shock.

'Why did you pretend to be asleep?' he asked.

'I don't know.' She couldn't think of any other answer.

'Do I frighten you so much?' He moved towards the bed.

Tamsin shook her head, and he sat down, as if suddenly weary. 'We can't go on like this,' he said.

'What—what do you mean?' she whispered. Had he seen it in her face? Was it so obvious? Please God, no, she thought.

'Fighting all the time, battling—the kids will sense the atmosphere soon. We must——' he hesitated, and she waited, her mind a blank, for what was to come, 'we must call a truce.'

It hadn't been what she expected. Restlessly, Tamsin stroked the coverlet. 'I know,' she answered. 'I'll try, if you will.'

Blaise looked at her. 'All I want is to be left alone to write,' he said, and she saw the lines of fatigue on his face.

'Then you shall be. I'm going to get up now. Are they downstairs?'

'Yes. They're playing in the lounge. I've lit a fire and given them their breakfast.' He looked at her, and it seemed as if he was about to say something else, then, without another word, Blaise got up and walked out. Something of the tension evaporated with his going, yet Tamsin was left with the strangest feeling that he too was strongly aware of it, and disturbed by it, yet puzzled.

She went over to close her door, and began to dress. Today she would take the children for a long walk, and tire both them and herself out. To have exchanged one problem for another was no solution to anything, and sometimes sheer physical exhaustion was the only antidote. And then, one way or another, she would try to find out how much longer they had to stay at the cottage.

It was easier not to think about Blaise when they were away from the cottage, walking briskly, the three of them, down a narrow country lane where there were no cars and no people, just the white snow all around, deadening sound, making it seem like another world. They had left him typing in the kitchen after lunch, and, wrapped up warmly, had set off. Tamsin had found a long stick at the start of their journey, and now, on a sudden idea, she stopped walking and said: 'Hold it! I've just thought of a game we can play.'

They looked at her, rosy-cheeked, eyes shining. 'What is it?' cried Paula.

'You'll see.' Tamsin began to mark holes in the snow at intervals of a foot or so. 'Have you ever seen people doing slalom on skis?' Peter frowned, so did Paula, and they looked at each other doubtfully. Tamsin laughed. She was some way ahead of them now, and the line of black cavities in the white snow stretched between them. 'It's where you have to run zig-zag without touching the marks I've made. And if you do,' she lowered her voice menacingly, 'you have to pay a forfeit.'

'What's a forfeit?' they both demanded, giggling.

'Well——' she hesitated, as if giving it much thought, 'you'd have to say a nursery rhyme or a poem—or sing a song. All right?'

They seemed to think it was a splendid idea, and had a brief argument as to whose turn it was to go first—and it was while they were doing so that Tamsin saw the car. She had heard it faintly, but the sound hadn't really registered; then it appeared, some distance behind them, on their road, driving slowly nearer and nearer. 'Stand in to the side,' she called out as she walked quickly back towards them. 'There's a car coming up. I'll probably have to do the holes again, unless it misses——' she stopped, because the car was slowing down, and it wasn't quite the same as the slowing-to-pass crawl—it seemed as though it was going to stop. She held their hands, and they waited, and then——

'Daddy! It's Daddy—look, Tammy!' Paula pulled away from Tamsin and ran towards the man who was getting out of the car, and Peter followed—and Tamsin ran after them, her eyes searching the car interior for another person. The man was alone. At least that was something. But oh, God, this was the worst thing that could have happened—and certainly in the worst place. There was no one at all, no other living creature, within sight. She took a deep breath, and prepared herself, as she reached the car, for what was to come.

The man slowly unfolded himself from the driving seat, and got out, hugging both his delighted children in a warm embrace before looking up slowly at Tamsin, and then smiling at her.

'Forgive me,' he said, 'but I had to see them.' He was tall and well built, with blue eyes in what Tamsin, in that first quick flash of seeing, could only describe as a gentle face. Yet he couldn't be gentle, could he? She had to keep a grip on reality, or she was lost. Her task was to protect them from him, not to smile back, as she found herself doing quite involuntarily.

'Look,' she began, 'you mustn't——'

'I know.' He gave them a last quick hug. 'Go and play for a moment, my children,' he said. 'I want to talk to this lady.' They looked at him, then at her.

'Tammy,' said Paula. 'That's Tammy—she's looking after us with Uncle Blaise while Mummy's ill.'

'Yes, my love, I know. Go and make some snowballs for me, will you?' They scampered off obediently. Tamsin found her strength.

'You must go,' she said. 'I'm sorry, but——'

'Please, just listen to me for a minute. Will you?' His blue eyes were steady on hers. 'I know how you're feeling at this moment. I can see the shock in your face—and you probably believe what others have told you about me. But you have no need to fear me. I love my children more than my life, and I mean them—and you—no harm. I wish only to speak to them—and to you—and then I'll go away again. There will be no battle—I'll not try to take them in the car. You have my word.'

'How can I believe you?' she said.

He handed her the car keys. 'Take those. I can't

drive away without them. And then perhaps you will listen to me, for I need help.'

She held the keys tightly. She wasn't sure if she was dreaming, but at least they were solid enough. 'Help?' she repeated his last word in a dazed way. 'What kind of help?'

'Will you sit in the car with me while we talk?'

She shook her head. 'No, I—we'll stay here.'

He smiled wearily. 'I understand. It's difficult—if you regard me as some kind of monster——'

'I don't. I don't regard you as anything—I don't know you. I only know that my job is to protect your children while their mother is ill.'

'And do you know what's wrong with her?'

'No. Does that matter? I'd probably be ill if I'd had to fight to get my children back——'

'Yes, that's what you've been told. But sometimes there are more truths than one—or to put it another way, there are other ways of looking at the same facts. And there we see a different picture.'

His words were confusing, yet she sensed a blazing sincerity in them, and she looked hard at him, and he nodded. 'Please, just listen—and then you'll see why I need help, and why I waited my chance, and followed you when I knew you were alone with the children.' He looked across to where they were busily scooping up handfuls of snow a few yards away, and Tamsin was surprised—and not a little moved—to see tears in his eyes. He looked back at her. 'After Paula was born, so soon after Peter, my wife suffered depression. It's natural enough, and fairly common, or so I'm told. We were living in Italy at the time—in Milan, where I work—and I was busy, too busy to see what was happening. I should have been more sympathetic and understanding, I see that now, when it is too late, but I thought she would snap out of it.'

He shrugged. 'What is done is done. If I could go back and have that time over again I would behave differently, but I can't—and now, perhaps, it's too late. There were quarrels. I was under pressure in my business, and that seemed more important—until the day I returned home from a business trip to find her gone with the children, and a note telling me she had gone back home to Scotland. So I followed. I left someone in charge of my shops—I run several department stores in northern Italy—and I told her that if it was what she wanted, we would live in Scotland. I love my wife very much, Tammy—I may call you Tammy, may I, please?' She nodded. 'Thank you. For a while that is what we did. We lived in Stirling, and I flew often to Italy and back, living two lives— and the pressure grew. She was a little better, and things improved—but I was feeling the strain now, and I suppose it showed. And then, last year, she lost the baby she was expecting, and because I was away in Rome at the time, she blamed me.'

He stopped, and Tamsin's heart went out to him at that moment. She could see the effort it was costing him to speak, yet she could not say anything. She had to hear his own words. She had to know the truth. Her instincts told her that that was precisely what she was hearing.

'Everything changed from that time on. The same thing happened that had happened after Paula's birth, only probably far worse, and while she was surrounded by her relatives, I had no one at all—and I saw gradually that they were closing ranks, that they regarded me as an unfeeling brute who thought only of money. How could I make them see? I tried, believe me, but it was impossible. Some of them had resented me marrying Fiona in the first place because I am a foreigner—from Milan—an Italian she had met on holiday, and they now hated me——'

Tamsin couldn't help herself. She had to know. 'Did Blaise—was he among the relatives who disliked you?'

His answer was stunning in its shock. 'I do not know him,' he said.

'You—you don't *know* him?'

He shook his head. 'I have met him, yes—once or twice briefly, but he lives and works in London. He is a writer, yes? We met at the wedding, and we got on well enough, and then once in London, with Fiona on our way through with the children—but do you think *he* would believe my story? I can imagine how he regards me.'

There was a brief silence. Then: 'But why—how did you expect me to believe you?' she asked.

'Because you are caring for my children. You are a woman, a stranger, and because I sense, in these few minutes of talking to you, that you are sympathetic and kind.'

Tamsin felt neither of those things, only totally confused. Yet out of the confusion something was growing. It was an awareness that she wanted desperately to help him. She looked at him. 'I believe all you say,' she answered slowly. 'But I'm not sure how I *can* help you.'

'If only I can see Fiona, and talk to her alone, without her being surrounded by her relatives—if I could do that, I would convince her that I love her truly. I know it.'

'You said yourself it's too late——'

'No. There *is* a chance, I see that now. A slim one, but a hope, nevertheless.'

'But you kidnapped your own children. Surely she must——'

'*No!* Is that what they said? How can anyone "kidnap" their own children? I took them away on a holiday because I thought that was the only way she would see sense—and come too. Only she didn't. She refused to go. I didn't realise how ill—mentally sick—she was when I left with them, because I was too stupid—and they let her come alone, after me, after some weeks, only by then it had blown up out of all proportion——' he stopped, as if despairing. 'You don't believe me, do you?' There was anguish in his eyes.

Tamsin nodded. 'Yes, I do. Oh yes, I believe you—and if I can, I'll help you.' The expression that came into his face at her words was almost painful to see. He looked like a man, who, near drowning, had suddenly been thrown a lifeline. He clasped her hands in his and shook them, and it was as though he were trying to speak, but couldn't.

Tamsin said gently: 'It's all right. Talk to your children for a few minutes while I think.'

Without a word he turned and left her. She watched him go to them, bend down, laughing with them as they picked up as many snowballs as they could carry, heard them talking. She watched them. She knew she was behaving in a totally irresponsible way. She was being paid to make sure that this man she stood watching was not allowed near her charges, she knew what she had been told, and exactly why she was looking after them—and she knew too that a terrible

injustice had been done, owing to a series of mis-
understandings that had multiplied until they were
seemingly insurmountable. And she knew in her heart
that she had to do something about it, but she hadn't
the faintest idea what.

It didn't seem to matter. What mattered was what
was happening at that precise moment: three human
beings were reunited after months of anguish. Tamsin
opened the door of the car and sat in the driving seat,
and began to think about everything. Life, two weeks
previously, when she had never even heard of Peter
and Paula and Blaise Torran, seemed to her now to
have been unbelievably smooth and uncomplicated.
And in less than a week it had turned topsy-turvy—all
because of what had seemed a fairly straightforward
job. She sighed. In a way, it all came back to one
man: Blaise. Hard, aggressive, ruthless, occasionally
charming, sensitive—a complex mixture wrapped up
in one human frame, and at the centre of it all. Blaise
Torran. She thought the name, and saw his face in her
mind's eye, and wondered if she would ever be cured
of him. And what did she do when she got back with
the children? Go up and say—look, I've had a chat
with their father and it's all been a mistake, so will you
get your sister Fiona down here and—she stopped.
She could imagine the reaction. And yet even thinking
that had given her the germ of an idea. Very slight,
intangible at the moment, but she would have to think
about it later on, when she was alone.

She took a deep breath. There was much to be
done, and said, and the time to start was now. She got
out of the car and walked towards the trio, and she
knew the first thing she had to do. It wouldn't be
easy—but it had to work.

They were nearly home, and dusk was falling, turning the snow to blue-grey, with darker shadows by the trees. Tamsin stopped, and held the children's hands tightly. 'Don't forget,' she said gently, 'what we have to do.'

'No, Tammy,' they chorussed obediently.

'It's our little secret, isn't it?'

Paula looked up, eyes shining. 'Yes. Daddy explained. We won't tell Uncle Blaise.'

'No, not yet. It's to be a surprise—soon, but not just yet.' She hated using the children in this way, but there was no alternative. If they let slip about the afternoon's events it would be disastrous all round. She had seen enough of Blaise Torran's temper to know who would be on the receiving end, and her plan would be in tatters before it had even begun. With any luck, if he was still writing, she could manage to keep them apart until bedtime, then whisk them off. And tomorrow was another day ... She touched the piece of paper in her pocket with Mario Zandradi's hotel telephone number on. She had promised to phone him when she could—when she knew anything at all. And he had promised to keep out of the way until she did so.

'Right, then, in we go. How about a special treat today? Tea by the fire while we watch television? That will give Uncle Blaise a chance to get on with his work, won't it?'

'And then he won't ask us what we've been doing, so we won't have to tell any fibs,' added Peter thoughtfully.

Smart child, Tamsin thought. 'That's it! Of course, we don't have to actually tell any fibs anyway,' she went on. 'You can tell him we played snowballs and had a long walk and saw some sheep—that's all true, you see. It's just—the other—is our secret for *now*.'

'Yes,' said Paula, 'our secret. Isn't it *lovely*?'

Tamsin opened the door. Her hand was trembling and it took her a few seconds to find the lock. Her mouth was dry and she felt like a prisoner about to be questioned, and she wished for a moment that she was anywhere but there. Then she took a deep breath and marched in. The hell with it! she thought. He can't kill me. 'In the lounge, children, switch on television, I'll go and make tea—that's it, give me your coats and I'll hang them up. Brr, it was cold outside, but it's lovely and warm in the lounge, I can hear the fire crackling from here——' she was babbling, she knew she was babbling, but for the moment she couldn't do anything about it. 'I shan't be a minute.' She walked into the kitchen and Blaise was there. He was still writing, and he looked up briefly.

'Had a good walk?'

'Yes. I'm having tea in there with them, so you can write in peace.' She busied herself with kettle and crockery, and her mind was working at top speed. An idea—the one so intangible before—was becoming stronger by the minute. She looked at Blaise, already lost in his own little world again, and she decided. 'I must phone my father, I'll not be a minute.'

She made sure the door was closed firmly when she went into the hall. From the lounge came the sound of shots, the thundering of hooves, and the racy background music of a Western. Tamsin picked up the telephone and dialled the number from the paper in her pocket. Moments later she was through. 'Mr Zandradi? It's Tammy Douglas here. I'd like to talk to you as soon as possible.' A pause as she listened. 'Tonight? Yes, I'll be there about eight-thirty, once the children are asleep. Goodbye.' The deed was done. She put the telephone down, and her heart was thudding. The clatter of Blaise's typewriter came from the kitchen, non-stop. Time for tea, and after that she would work out what she would tell him. Just as long as the children were fast asleep before she went, there would be no hitches. It would all be rather simple.

CHAPTER EIGHT

'It was good of you to come, Tammy, I am so grateful.' Mario Zandradi smiled at Tamsin across the round table in the hotel lounge. 'A drink for you?'

'I'd better not—I'm driving.' She smiled back at him. 'I'd like a coffee if it's possible, though. I don't want to be away too long. I told Blaise I was going for a drive and to post some letters.' She looked at her watch.

'I understand, of course. You have some idea—some plan?' He signalled a passing waiter as he spoke. 'Two coffees, please.'

'I can't ask Blaise how best to approach his sister—but you can tell me. I'm going to try and persuade her to come down here—I don't know how, yet, that's what I want to talk over with you. How ill is she? Do you think she'd be able to travel?'

'Yes, I think so. If she had good enough reason. Have you talked to her yet on the phone?'

Tamsin shook her head. 'No, but I'll find some excuse tomorrow. It will establish a link. Then, when Blaise is out shopping——' she shrugged, 'I'll take it from there.'

'It won't be easy.'

'I know, but I'm going to try. Just tell me everything you can about her, her interests, the sort of things she would enjoy chatting about—it will help

120

me to build up a picture of her in my mind——' she hesitated. His blue eyes were warm and friendly upon her.

'Oh yes! If only it would work! And there is no reason not. You are clever, Tammy, I sense it——' he paid the waiter and offered Tamsin a cigarette. 'No? You will permit me to smoke then?'

'Of course. Please, don't raise your hopes too much—but if I could make some notes—I find it easier.' She took out her diary, found the blank note pages at the back, and held her pen poised. 'Fire away.'

'Right. Well, first——' he talked for twenty minutes with barely a pause, and Tamsin's hand ached when he had finished. But it was all down on paper, and her confidence was steadily growing.

'Are you sure I cannot accompany you home in my car?' he said, as she put the diary away. 'To make sure?'

'No. It's not far, really. I must go now. I'll phone again as soon as I can.' Then she remembered. Mario Zandradi saw the change in her expression, the sudden flare of alarm in her eyes, and said quickly:

'What is it? Something is wrong?'

'No, I just remembered. When I phoned you—I'd told Blaise I was going to phone my father. I meant to immediately afterwards, but I forgot—is there a telephone here somewhere?' She looked around her. 'I'll call him now, in case.'

'Of course, in the reception hall. Come.' He led her out of the lounge. 'You want silver?'

She was already fumbling in her purse. 'No, thanks, I have enough. I'll leave you here. After I've called Dad I'll get off back to the cottage.' She shook hands with him. 'Don't worry, please. I'm going to do all I can.'

'I know you are. Thank you. I'll wait for your call. If you need me—after you have phoned your father, I shall be in the lounge having a drink. *Arrivederci,* Tammy.'

He waited until she was in the telephone booth before waving and turning away. Tamsin dialled her father's number and waited impatiently for him to answer. And until he answered, she hadn't realised that she was going to have to lie to him too, as well as to Blaise.

'Hello, Dad? It's me, Tam. How is——'

'Tamsin? What's going on, love? And why are you ringing from a pip-pip box? Blaise said——'

'Oh *no!*' her cry of anguish echoed down the line, effectively stopping him. 'Have you phoned?'

'Well, of course I did. And he said you'd already rung me, only——'

'Look, I can explain *that.*' She hoped she would be able to. 'Did he sound—er—annoyed?'

'Not particularly. What the hell goes? Where *are* you?'

'In a pub.' That at least was the truth.

'Hmm. He said you'd gone to post letters or something.'

'Well, yes, only I popped in for a coffee——'

'In a pub?'

'Well, it's a hotel as well——'

'Come off it, love. I know you well enough to recognise a certain shiftiness in your voice.'

Tamsin sighed a huge sigh. 'It's very difficult. I didn't want him to know where I was, that's all. I met a friend——'

'A friend? You don't know anyone up there, do you?'

It was getting worse. She felt like a traitor. She *was* a traitor; she was effectively going against all her training by having spoken to Mario Zandradi in the first place—and compounding the treachery by not reporting it to her father. Then an image of the children laughing with *their* father rose in her mind. That did it. Nothing could alter the rightness of that. Her father would understand—eventually—but not yet. 'Have you forgotten Sandra? I bumped into her when we were out for a walk today—what a coincidence! And I didn't tell *him* because he's an arrogant, nosey beast, and quite frankly I didn't see why I should.' She pushed in another coin as the pips went. 'Anyway, I'm off back now. Anything to report?'

'No. Have you?' An innocent enough question. And if only he could guess the truth!

'Not much. I taped an interview with Blaise last night, about work, you know, and it turned out quite well. He was particularly interested in the Brewer case——'

'Hah! I can understand why! Why is he an arrogant beast?'

'He just *is*. But we get on all right—and the children are super. Good as gold most of the time, and quite entertaining——' it was so much easier to talk about them than about their uncle. 'They enjoy all the games, and we have occasional reading sessions, you know, and they're no trouble at all—and I must have a word with their mother some time, to see if there's anything she gives them in winter, like vitamin pills——' she babbled on until her father interrupted her with :

'Okay, love, I get the message. I'm sure you're taking care of everything extremely well, but I have to go now. I've got your Uncle Charles coming over for a game of chess, and——'

'Oops, sorry! I'll let you go. Give him my love. I'll get back now—'bye, love.'

' 'Bye. Take care.'

'I will.' She hung up, feeling wretched. At least that was done. Back to the cottage. An early night was called for, perhaps a read in bed, and then a good think about the bizarre situation that had arisen. And it would be a means of keeping out of *his* way. She set off to drive back to the cottage in a slightly easier frame of mind. Blaise would be too busy typing to remember the slight error of the telephone call. So she thought. But she was wrong.

Something in the atmosphere should have warned her when she walked into the kitchen—but it didn't, because she was too busy trying to be extremely casual. The kettle was on, just about to boil. She went over to it and added another beaker to the one already standing at the side, turned to Blaise and asked: 'Are you having coffee or tea?'

'Tea. I forgot to ask—before. You got through to your father all right when you phoned?' She didn't like the way he said the words, and the fact that she knew why didn't help at all. She didn't like the expression on his face either, come to that, but there wasn't much she could do about it.

'Didn't I say? I couldn't get through to him. Has he phoned?'

'He has. Then who did you phone instead?'

'Does it matter? It's really none of your business,' she retorted smartly.

'It is when you deliberately lie. You only dialled the once—so you didn't even try to get him.' For a moment her heart stopped. How much had he heard?

'You should have come into the hall with me,' she answered angrily, 'it would have been more comfortable there than having your ear pressed against the door.'

'Don't be so damned flippant. You can hardly miss hearing the dialling sound here.'

'You should be a detective, not a writer,' she said icily. He couldn't have heard her voice—or he would have said by now. He was not a man to bottle up his feelings—and yet she must tread with care. There was a dangerously explosive quality to him. He stood up now and came towards her.

'You can entertain your men friends here, if that's what you want,' he said, his voice harsh. 'I'm broad-minded——'

'I don't know what you mean!' Tamsin whirled away and turned the kettle off. She felt almost sick with shock. Had he guessed?

'You liar. You've gone white as a sheet——'

'Only because I find you so offensive. You are deliberately insulting——'

'And you soon get over your broken heart, don't you? Or was it the errant Nigel that you met?'

She turned on him, anger and relief making a heady mixture. He didn't know about Mario Zandradi—but he could not have been more objectionable if he had tried. 'How *dare* you!' she breathed. 'You are *despicable*!'

'I've not even started yet. God, you had me fooled with that weepy act. I'll bet you enjoyed every minute of it—is that how you get *your* kicks?' He was even more furious than she. Even in the midst of her own wrath, Tamsin was strongly aware of that. The air vibrated with their anger. She wanted to hit him, to hurt him, to lash out at him and see the pain—yet she steeled herself, for he was at flashpoint, more angry than she had ever seen any man—and she didn't know why.

'Get out of my way,' she said, voice low and trembling. 'I'm going to bed. I'm not standing here listening to you——' She moved as if to go past him, but he caught her arms and held her in a grip of steely hardness.

'You're not going anywhere.'

'Let me *go*!'

'Until you've told me the truth.'

'You're *hurting* my arms——'

'I want to hurt you. Oh God, I want to hurt you——' And, the next moment, his lips came down on hers in a kiss of savage intensity, knocking the breath from her body as she was crushed against the sink, powerless to move, numbed and nearly insensible. She tried to speak, but his mouth covered hers, and she tasted the saltness of his kiss, felt the hardness of his muscular body pressing against her, then his hands moved, and she felt the wild excitement within him, the roughness of his caress, the sheer, violent physical strength of him against which she had absolutely no defence, none at all. Her own strength was ebbing away; as his mouth moved to her neck, his hands to her breast, she found sufficient power to mùrmur:

'No, please—you're——'

She heard as if from a great distance his voice saying something, but she scarcely heard for the pounding of blood in her ears. Suddenly she was filled with a warm, treacherous excitement. He was going to make love to her, and there was nothing to stop him, for she was past any effort at defence, and when, the next moment, his mouth found hers again, she responded, trembling, knowing that this was what she had been waiting for since that first moment she had seen him ... knowing ... knowing now why she had been so afraid of him, and no longer caring. Then came a loud thud, and somewhere a child screamed in fear—and the spell was broken.

Tamsin heard Blaise say something. 'The children,' she whispered, 'one of them——' But he had already gone. Tamsin stood there, straightening her dishevelled clothes, and managed to find the strength to walk to the door. She felt bruised all over, as if the whole of her body ached, and her breathing was ragged as if she had run a long way. She took a deep shuddering breath and walked unsteadily along the hall and up the stairs.

It was Peter who had called out, and woken his sister, and Blaise was in with them talking softly, soothing—a different man from the one minutes previously. Tamsin stood there watching him for a moment before going over to the window where Peter pointed. She looked out, to see the fall of snow on the lower roof outside, and her mouth trembled. 'It was only snow falling from the roof, Peter,' she said.

'It banged—it frightened me,' he whispered. 'I was dreaming about Daddy and Mummy——' Tamsin was instantly alert. Any moment now, in their half sleeping state, they might say something that would ruin everything. And she had nearly forgotten.

'It's all right, love, I'll stay with you for a while. Would you like a warm drink?'

Paula nodded. 'Drinking chocolate, please.'

'Me too. Don't go away, Tammy.'

'I'll make it.' Blaise got up and looked at Tamsin, and she looked away. She let him go, and sat down on Peter's bed.

'I'll sleep in here tonight if you like,' she said. The moment of madness had passed. Aching and raw though she still was, sanity had returned. She had wanted Blaise to make love to her because she loved him—but she knew that his motive had been only the most savage punishment he knew in his great anger. And it had so nearly happened. Then she would have had to leave—and nothing would have been solved. She shivered, suddenly cold. 'There's room for you both in one bed,' she said. 'You can sleep top to tail if you like.'

They were both interested, fright forgotten. 'What's that?' they demanded.

Tamsin laughed. 'I'll show you,' she said. She began to loosen the bedclothes at the foot of Paula's bed. 'We put a pillow there, and one of you sleeps upside down, as it were. Your toes might meet in the middle, but it's very comfy and cosy.'

'Bags I at the bottom!'

'No. Me, Tammy, please——'

'Whoa! We'll decide in a minute when you've had your drinks.' She added briskly: 'I'll go and fetch my pillow in. Shan't be a moment.'

She heard Blaise coming up the stairs as she carried

her pillow in from her room, and he looked up and saw her. 'I'm staying with them tonight,' she said.

He looked at her as he reached her. She saw what was in his eyes, and she couldn't look away. 'No,' he answered harshly.

'Yes.' She turned away and went into the bedroom and flung her pillow on Peter's bed. 'Here's your drinks. Careful not to spill any, now.'

'Tell us a story, Uncle Blaise,' asked Paula.

'Please,' added Peter. Blaise looked at them, and seemed about to say no.

'What a good idea,' said Tamsin. 'I'll go and get ready for bed while you do.' She went out, closing the door softly behind her. She heard his voice as she stood just outside on the landing, and put her hand to her mouth, feeling the tenderness there, and wondering what was going on in his mind at that moment. His anger would be of a different kind now, and she had seen what she had seen in his eyes, and knew why he didn't want her to sleep with the children. Then she crept quietly along to her room. Life would not be made easier by what had happened. He had probably never been thwarted before. It would be like living on the edge of a volcano ... It decided her. For the rest of her stay at the cottage she would sleep with the children. There was nothing Blaise could do about that. Although she was no longer sure about anything where Blaise Torran was concerned. And she had forgotten completely her puzzlement over his anger.

She awoke in the middle of the night, and remembered it, and thought about it for several minutes before drifting off to sleep again. In that brief moment before sleep claimed her, she recognised what she had seen on his face when he had accused her of meeting another man—it was jealousy. By the morning she had forgotten all about it.

There was a brittle awareness now in everything that happened. It was as though the incidents of the previous night had sharpened her senses, turning them to a fine pitch of consciousness. When she went downstairs at eight, Blaise was already up, sitting at his typewriter. She took a deep breath, surprised, and felt the instant tension in the room.

'Have you had coffee?' she asked.

'No. I've been too busy writing to make any.' He was dressed, but he hadn't shaved. He looked as though he hadn't slept either, which prompted her to say:

'Don't tell me you've been up all night?'

'Would it make any difference to you if I had?'

So that's the way of it, she thought, and was almost amused. 'I couldn't give a damn,' she answered, and nearly meant it. 'You can sit here typing day and night as far as I'm concerned.' She put the kettle on. 'I'll make you a cup. You look as though you need one.' Then she smiled, because one thing was certain: the powerful, aggressive Blaise Torran was not feeling his best. It made her, oddly enough, feel much better herself.

She opened the back door and threw out some crusts of stale bread, had a look at the snowy garden, then came back in.

He suddenly slammed down a book he had been referring to on the table. 'Do you have to leave the bloody door wide open while you feed the damned birds?' he demanded. Tamsin glanced at him, saw the whiteness round his mouth, the tiredness in his eyes, and blinked.

'Good gracious, I'm sorry,' she exclaimed. 'I didn't realise you were cold. Would you like a blanket round you?'

He stood up. 'I'm going to bed—now you're up.'

'Yes, I should.' She smiled. 'It'll be rather difficult setting the table round that clutter.' She touched the kettle. 'Coffee will be ready in a moment. You might as well take it up with you.'

'I sure as hell wouldn't ask you to bring it up,' he said grittily.

She frowned. 'I shan't say another word. Obviously everything I say is wrong,' and she began to move very quietly, not quite on tiptoe, but managing to imply that she was making the effort. She handed him his beaker without a word, and he took it from her and began to walk away. She let him get nearly to the door, then:

'And I'll put *all* your things away tidily for you, don't worry,' she said in soothing tones.

Blaise muttered something brief and unprintable, turned round, put down the beaker, and began gathering up the pile of typescript. Only his movements weren't as sure as they might have been, and the next moment everything was scattered on the floor. Tamsin couldn't help herself. She burst out laughing—then was silent as he rounded on her. He towered over her, and she saw the darkness of the anger on his face and caught her breath. She saw his fists clench and waited numbly for him to strike her, eyes wide with fear. He looked as if he might—then she saw pain in his eyes, and it was frightening to see, more frightening than if he had hit her.

'Oh, God!' He put his hand to his face, the words wrenched from him in anguish, and Tamsin reached out to touch his arm.

'What's the——' he pushed her arm away savagely and she backed, regretting her impulsive action. 'I'm sorry,' she breathed. 'I'm sorry I *touched* you——' her mouth trembled. This was more frightening than anything else that had been, ever. She wanted to move away, but she was unable to. She felt as if it wasn't really happening, as if she were an onlooker herself to some scene in a play; or a dream—or a nightmare. 'I'll pick them up.' The words came with difficulty, forced out.

'Don't touch them. I'll do it.' He raised his hand, and she flinched—then he said: 'Did you think I was going to hit you?'

'Yes. Weren't you?'

His face was white with fatigue and the remains of the terrible anger she had seen, yet she faced him because a sense of inevitability washed over her, and she could not—would not—run away, or she was lost. 'I don't know.' His lips barely moved; and she sensed the terrible pressure that was in him.

'Then why don't you, and get it over with?' she demanded. 'I can't—I can't s-stand here all day——'

He shook his head, and it seemed that he swayed slightly, and a tide of anger rose within Tamsin, overwhelming her. 'Then get out and leave me alone,' she shouted. 'Go on, get out!' Blaise put out his hand, and she thought it was to silence her, and struck it away from her as all the pent up frustration bubbled over inside her and she pushed him. 'Get *out*!'

His head jerked up, and his eyes burned into her. 'I'm going,' he blazed back. 'I don't want to be in the same room as you—you scheming little b——' Tamsin cut off his words by hitting him as hard as she was able, then in a frenzy she hit him again, then stood back, panting, realising—seeing the violence in him, trembling—but he turned away without a word and walked out of the room.

She was alone. She wanted to run after him and punish him for what he had done. She wanted again to hurt him—then she remembered his face, and knew, then, that somehow she had already hurt him enough. Sinking to her knees, her eyes full of tears so that the papers were all blurred, she began to pick them up from the floor.

Blaise had left his coffee. She poured it down the sink and then drank her own. She had to speak to his sister soon, the sooner the better, for she could not stay much longer in the same house as Blaise Torran. Not if she was to keep her sanity. When everything had been put away, she sat down at the table, completely drained of energy. She hoped that the children would sleep late. There were no sounds from upstairs, all was quiet. And gradually, as the minutes passed, she began to feel calmer. She would feel better for food inside her, she knew that. After a time, she got up and began to make breakfast for herself. By the time the children woke up and came down to tell her all about how funny it was sleeping feet to feet, she was nearly back to normal.

Her opportunity to telephone Fiona Zandradi came later in the afternoon when Blaise went out in her car with the children. She watched the blue Mini vanish out of sight, then went and picked up the telephone. Her mouth was dry with apprehension, and she took a glass of water from the kitchen, drank some, put it on the table and picked up the receiver.

She had planned her opening words. What happened after that depended on the response of the woman she was calling. And Tamsin had another method for helping her to cope with difficult situations, a kind of positive thinking that had enabled her to sail through many tricky jobs. She did it now, putting down the receiver while she slowly counted to twenty, breathing deeply and calmly and putting in her mind a mental image of the situation she wanted to happen—the successful reunion of Mario Zandradi with his wife. She pictured a smiling couple, together with the two children, and held the picture in her mind as she finished counting, picking up the receiver, and began to dial the number.

'Hello? May I speak to Mrs Zandradi? This is Tamsin Douglas.'

The voice was soft, the Scottish accent more pronounced than the children's. 'Speaking—is everything all right, Miss Douglas?'

'Oh, fine, just fine. But I thought I'd ring you, Mrs Zandradi, to ask if the children needed any vitamin supplements—you see, I've got several nieces and nephews, and I remembered that my sister-in-law doses them at this time of the year—and it's pretty cold here at the moment. I don't know what it's like your end——' she paused, knowing that in the reply she would be able to tell how her call was being received.

'Och, it's terrible here too, we've had lots of snow. Yes, it's very kind of you to call, and I had forgotten. Well, I usually give them malt and cod liver oil and——' Tamsin noted down what the other said, and sensed the gradual relaxing of the woman as she talked. She sensed something else too: that Fiona Zandradi badly needed someone to talk to. So do I, she thought wryly, but her need's greater than mine. She winced as she thought of the cost of the call, but that wasn't as important as what was happening. For Tamsin had confirmation of something else she had hoped for—their mother was missing Peter and Paula desperately. It came over in the anxious enquiries as to what they were doing, were they good, did they play happily, were they eating well?

'They're fine, but they miss you—I can tell. It takes a woman to know these things, doesn't it? What fun it would be if you could come and surprise them.' She crossed her fingers as she said it.

'I've been ill—and there's a court case—you see, Miss Douglas——'

'Tamsin, please call me Tamsin,' she said. 'Or Tammy—that's what the children call me.'

'Tammy, of course—you see, I've been ill—all the worry. They needed to get away, they've been through so much. I don't know if Blaise has told you——' No, Tamsin thought, but your husband has, and I know now that I can help.

'I do know, Mrs Zandradi, but you see, I'd be here as well, to help you. You wouldn't have to do anything at all, except play with your children. And I need someone to talk to—you see, I have a slight problem——' Tamsin listened to herself saying the words with faint horror, but she couldn't stop herself. Something told her she was saying exactly the right thing, the one thing that would tip the balance. '—I've rather fallen in love with your brother—and I'm afraid—I'm afraid——' she stopped.

'Oh dear! Oh *dear*, Tammy, that *is* a problem!' But could that actually be a hint of laughter in the other's tones? A kind of relief at someone else actually having problems too? Tamsin's heart did a flip.

'Oh, I'm sorry—I don't know what made me say that! Mrs Zandradi——'

'Fiona.'

'Fiona—thank you.' It had worked! Somehow it *had* worked. 'I shouldn't have blurted that out, but I've no one to talk to, you see——'

'And there's nothing like another woman, is there?' She gave a deep sigh. 'I'm surrounded by well-meaning relatives here—believe me, Tammy, you don't know how I long for someone to talk to as well sometimes. I can't think straight——'

'Please, Fiona—please come. I can help you,' said Tamsin.

There was a long silence, so long that she feared they had been cut off. Then: 'Yes, I think you can.' It was only faint, as if Fiona Zandradi had made a tremendous effort in saying it.

Tamsin closed her eyes. 'Then—will you?'

Again a pause. 'Yes, I will.'

'That's wonderful! When? Now—today?'

There was a burst of laughter, heartening to hear. 'Oh, I'm glad you're looking after my children! You must be a lot of fun to be with. I'll come tomorrow, before anyone can persuade me to change my mind— and they'll try, believe me. I'll get a train from Glasgow—you'll have to tell me the nearest main station and I'll——'

'I'm going to check up now—and I'll meet you as well. That will be a surprise for them, because I'll not say a word. Can I ring you back in, say, ten minutes?'

'Yes. I'll phone this end as well—thank you, Tammy. I think you've saved my life, if you know what I mean!'

Tammy grinned. 'I know—I'll call you. Ten minutes. 'Bye.'

She hung up, then did a little dance along the hall in sheer exuberance, all cares forgotten—well, almost. Then, sobering, she picked up the telephone, flipped through the phone book for British Rail enquiries, and began to dial.

CHAPTER NINE

TAMSIN waited at York station for the train to come in. It was just after lunch, and she had left Blaise with the children at the house, told him she had somewhere urgent to go, and set off. She had hardly been able to contain her secret the previous evening, and it must have shown on her face, for she could see that he was puzzled by her behaviour. She didn't care what he thought any more. The scene of the morning had numbed her feelings towards him, and she made sure she was never alone with him.

Nor would she be again. Because once Fiona was settled in, and the plan was successfully completed, she, Tamsin, would leave. She walked up the platform, hands in pockets, shivering slightly in the cold air as she waited. Ten minutes to go, that was all. Mario Zandradi's reaction, when she had telephoned him immediately after her second call to Fiona, had been stunned. He had refused to believe her at first, begging her not to joke with him—until she had managed to convince him she spoke the truth. Then he had let out a shout of delight that had nearly shattered the telephone—and Tamsin's eardrum—and been almost incoherent in his thanks. She had made him promise to wait for her call, then, hearing the car return, had said goodbye and hung up.

Now, hearing the train, she said a little prayer, and

waited, watching it snake along, nearer and nearer
noisier and noisier—until, with a great clank and hiss-
ing of brakes, it stopped. They had described each
other over the telephone—amid mutual laughter—and
Tamsin watched the people pour off and filter through
the barrier, fanning out in all directions to be greeted
by relatives and friends, young and old, men and
women, families—then she saw her, the tall fair-haired
too-thin woman who stood holding a small case at the
other side of the barrier. Tamsin waved, the woman
waved back, then she was through, and they were
shaking hands, and smiling at each other.

'Hello, Tammy,' said Fiona. 'You described yourself well—I'm delighted to meet you.'

'And I you. Shall we go for a coffee before we set
off? We've an hour's drive ahead of us.'

'Yes. I'd like to talk, before we get there.' Tamsin
picked up Fiona's case, ignoring her protest.

'Look, you've not been well—and I promised to
look after you, and I'm going to.'

Fiona laughed. 'I feel better already. How are they?
You don't know how I've missed them—oh, Tammy,
if only I could tell you——' she stopped.

'You can,' Tamsin answered quietly. 'But I'm beginning to have a good idea anyway. You can tell
me—and be sure it won't go any further.' They
walked in comfortable silence to the buffet and after
seating themselves, drank their coffee while they
talked. Then it all came pouring out—Fiona's version,
which oddly enough, wasn't so much different from
Mario's, and only served to show the already aware
Tamsin just how slight could be the original cause of
great unhappiness. Her heart warmed towards Blaise's
sister as it had to her husband only days previously.

Fiona's face was beautiful and gentle, yet she was too pale, too fragile-looking.

'The job I had to get away!' she said, pulling a face. 'But I'd made up my mind—because you'd made it up for me, I suppose, and I wouldn't be budged. So here I am.' She smiled. 'It's lovely having a big family, Tammy, but sometimes they can be too close—too demanding.' She sipped her coffee. 'I know now why Blaise broke away from them when he was younger. He's always been very much a loner—I'm sorry, I've just remembered. Here am I pouring out my troubles, and you've got problems of your own. I'm afraid I'm going to sound terribly rude, but what on earth made you fall for *him*?'

'I wish I knew.' Tamsin shrugged, as though that would ease it. 'I know it hurts though—I'm glad you're here, Fiona. Perhaps you'll make me see sense.'

'I doubt it,' Fiona smiled. 'I've not been so clever myself, have I?'

Tamsin, knowing what she did, looked at her and smiled back. 'I think we're going to have time for lots of talks,' she answered. She looked at her watch. 'Perhaps we'd better be setting off. I'll tell you something before we do—a little confession. I didn't really phone you about vitamins—I just needed an excuse to talk to you.'

'And I know why now,' said Fiona. 'And I'm glad you did.'

Oh no, you don't, thought Tamsin. Not yet, anyway. But you will—soon. 'So am I,' she answered instead, and led the way out to her car.

'Wait there,' said Tamsin. 'I'll go in first and tell them. They're not going to believe me—but I want to see their faces when you walk in. I'll leave the door open.' She shut her car door and opened the door of the cottage. She could hear voices from the lounge and went in to see the three of them playing Ludo, sitting on the floor. The children looked up, Blaise didn't.

'I've got a surprise for you,' said Tamsin. Peter and Paula jumped to their feet and scampered over.

'What is it?'

'Not what—who. Guess.'

'It's Mummy! It's Mummy!' and at that Blaise looked up, his expression showing clearly what his thoughts were. I shall enjoy this, thought Tamsin.

'Yes, you're right, it is. Come with me.' Blaise got to his feet and said:

'Don't you think it's rather a sick joke to tell children——' and at that moment Fiona walked in, knelt in front of her children and gathered them into her arms. Tamsin looked at Blaise, saw the utter disbelief on his face, said: 'I'll go and make us all a drink,' and walked out.

She heard him come into the kitchen, heard too the laughter cut off as he closed the door, but she didn't turn round from where she was busying herself with the cups. She felt a warm satisfied glow that not even he could take away, whatever he said or did. She was prepared for almost anything, but not for what he actually said.

'How did you do it?' he asked, and he still looked stunned. She smiled gently.

'I phoned her,' she said. 'We talked, and we talked —quite a lot—and I told her the children were missing her, which is true—and—it sort of seemed natural for her to come down.'

'I don't believe it,' he said.

'She's real enough,' Tamsin answered. 'And she's here, so it doesn't really matter whether you believe it or not. I know she's not well, but I'm going to look after her and see she gets plenty of food and rest.' She made a potful of tea and began to pour milk into the cups. 'Will you find a tray?' she asked him. 'It will make it easier to carry everything in.'

'Why?' he asked.

'So that I can put the cups on it.'

'Not the tray, dammit! Why did you want her down here?' She turned to look at him then, wondering if she would see suspicion on his face—wondering if he guessed ... But he didn't.

'Because she's better off with her children,' she retorted. 'And because—since you've asked, as soon as she's fit and able to look after them, I can leave—and because I feel *safer* with another woman in the house, and I'm sure you don't need to ask why for *that*, do you?'

He turned away without another word and walked out. She watched him go and her feelings were mixed. She found the tray herself, poured out the tea, and carried it in. There was a busy time ahead of her, in more ways than one, and she felt equal to it. She nearly dropped the tray as she entered the lounge, for she remembered something that had completely gone from her mind. Steadying it, she put it down, said: 'Will you excuse the children for a moment, Fiona—I want to have a word with them in the kitchen. Do get your tea, please—come on, children.'

Puzzled, obedient, they followed her out, leaving Blaise and his sister alone. Tamsin closed the door. 'You remember out little secret, children—about your daddy?' They nodded. 'Well, it's still got to be a secret—but just for a little while longer. Now, will you *promise*, because it's very important.'

Paula hugged her. 'We love you, Tammy,' she said, 'and you brought us our mummy, and of course we'll keep the secret 'cos it's going to be a nice surprise, isn't it, like Mummy came just now?'

'Precisely.' Tamsin sighed a relieved sigh. 'I see you understand. All right now, we'll go back—and oh! tell you what—we'll go and buy Mummy a present tomorrow, shall we? That's another secret.' And one which, when hinted at, would explain the reason for their disappearance to the kitchen. I'm getting very devious, she thought, I only hope I don't get myself into a tangle with it all. She took their hands and went back into the lounge with them.

Fiona's presence altered the atmosphere tremendously. Later that evening, when the children were at last, reluctantly, tucked up in bed, and Blaise was typing in the kitchen, she and Tamsin sat by a crackling fire in the lounge and relaxed. A bottle of wine stood on the table, and Fiona stretched sleepily. 'I'm so tired,' she admitted, 'but I feel better than I have for months.'

'You can have an early night,' said Tamsin. 'I've given you my bed, so you'll have undisturbed sleep,' and she explained her reason for moving in with the children two nights previously. At least she explained the obvious reason. Not the other one. Nothing could ever be said about that to anyone. 'And you can have breakfast in bed in the morning if you like.'

Fiona began to laugh. 'I'm sure all this wasn't in your contract,' she protested, shaking her head. 'What can I say?'

'Nothing,' answered Tamsin firmly. 'It's all part of

the Douglas Agency service. More wine?'

'No, thanks, I've had enough. But I'd love a cup of tea before I go to bed. Can I make you one as well?'

'I'll make it. You sit there and do nothing.'

'You'll have me getting fat!'

'Good,' answered Tamsin as she went out. She made tea for three, put some biscuits on a plate, deposited Blaise's tea on his table without a word, and left him alone again.

'Do you want to talk about him?' asked Fiona gently.

Tamsin sighed. 'Not tonight. Besides, in a funny way, your being here helps. I don't know how, or why, but it does.'

'That's good. Only—I can't explain, but he seems different somehow.'

'In what way?'

Fiona regarded Tamsin thoughtfully. 'I don't know. He looks at you—I've seen him, and he seems——' she paused.

'Go on,' prompted Tamsin. 'Don't stop there—he looks as if he'd like to murder me—or what?'

Fiona gave an odd little smile. 'That's not how I'd have put it, no,' she said slowly. 'He looks—lost, somehow, and that, believe me, is not the way Blaise usually looks.'

A little shiver ran up Tamsin's spine. Lost—what a strange word for Fiona to use! People like Blaise were never lost. They always knew exactly where they were going, and what they wanted. And they usually got it. And that's why I'm very glad you're here, she thought, because he very nearly got what he wanted the other night.

'What is it?' asked Fiona very gently. 'You can tell me.'

'Nothing. I was just thinking—a man like Blaise, he's different from ordinary men, isn't he? Perhaps you can't see it because you're his sister, but he's a very powerful personality.'

'Och, I know that well. He is that all right! He was let down badly by a woman some years ago, and he's hated women ever since—or avoided them, rather——'

'I didn't know that,' said Tamsin. It explained a lot, but it didn't help. She sipped the hot tea.

'He doesn't talk about it, ever. But it does help *me* to understand him—with my problems.' Tamsin looked into her cup. Perhaps now was the moment. It wouldn't hurt—not if she asked it carefully.

'Do you hate your husband, Fiona?' She almost regretted the question as she saw the painful flush that rose in the other's cheeks, and said quickly: 'I'm sorry, I shouldn't have——'

'It's all right. I told you I could talk to you. To anyone else I would say—yes. To you I must be absolutely honest. I—I don't know—I'm so confused——' Fiona stopped. Tamsin put her hand on her arm.

'It's all right, love. I asked it for a reason.'

Something flared in Fiona's eyes. Was it hope? 'What reason?' she whispered.

'The children—from things they've said—love him a lot. But I think you know that, don't you?'

'Yes.' It was barely a whisper of sound. 'Yes—but it's all too late—much too late. I can't——' she bit her lip.

'You can't what? Go back?'

Fiona shook her head. 'No. There's too much bit-
terness—too much been said, and done.' She put her
cup down, and it was clear what state her nerves were
in by the way she clasped and unclasped her hands.
Tamsin felt such an intense surge of pity for her that
it was nearly overwhelming. If only she could tell
her—but she must not. Not yet. It must not be
rushed.

'If you want to talk, go ahead. If you don't that's
fine. That's what I'm here for.'

'You're marvellous—I don't know how to thank
you enough already, Tammy, and you know something? I feel as if I've got something to look forward
to tomorrow. That's a new feeling for me, believe me.'

'You have. Bacon and eggs in bed! Porridge too if
you want.'

'I didn't mean that!' But she managed to laugh all
the same. 'Is it all right if I go up now? You don't
mind?'

'No, I'm tired myself. Come on, I'll show you your
room. I've moved things out to give you some drawer
space—I think you'll find it comfortable.'

'I'll say goodnight to Blaise. Does he write *all* the
time?'

'Most of it. I'll be upstairs. Just come up when
you're ready.'

Half an hour later, Tamsin was in bed herself. She lay
awake, her brain too full of thoughts to be able to
sleep. She heard Blaise's quiet footsteps on the stairs,
then soon after, his door closing. So he too was having
an early night. Her heart ached in sudden pain for
him, for loving and hating him at the same time, and

she closed her eyes, seeing his face, seeing every detail with great clarity. And some woman, perhaps years ago, had hurt him badly. We've all been hurt, she thought—but at least there'll be one happy ending when Fiona and Mario are together again. She smiled to herself in the darkness, imagining how she would set about it, wondering about Mario's feelings—her fellow conspirator—knowing that his wife was so near. Perhaps he wasn't sleeping either. I should phone him, she thought, and meet him for a drink, and we could discuss our plans. And on that thought, she drifted off into sleep.

She woke early the following morning and lay for a moment before remembering. Everywhere was silent. The two children fast asleep in their makeshift bed, curled up snugly and warm. Shivering a little, Tamsin pulled on her dressing gown and went down to tidy the house and light the fire. Today might be the day. There was a glorious uncertainty about it all, and it was a challenge, because the uncertainty was not in whether everything would work out right, but when.

Humming a little song, she began to clear the ashes from the fireplace in the lounge. When she had set the fire she would have breakfast, then clean the kitchen … she made her plans, and the day stretched comfortably ahead, and she began to feel happy for the first time in days. Carrying the ash pan carefully, so as not to spill hot ashes on the carpets, she made her way out to the kitchen, unbolted the door, and went outside to the dustbin. It was icy cold, the snow glinted with silver crystals, and nothing stirred. Turning back to the house, she stepped on a slippery patch and skidded several inches before falling heavily on her back. For a moment she lay, too winded to try and move, then attempted to get up. Pain shot up her foot, making her cry out. It was so cold, so icy cold, and it bit through her dressing gown and she felt the numbness seeping into her bones and knew she must get in. Hot tears filled her eyes, not of pain but of frustration. Nothing must go wrong now. Not now, of all days. Very carefully, she eased herself up to her feet. Her right leg hurt terribly when she tried to put her weight on it, and her face was hot with the sheer effort of standing upright. She tried to hop, but the jarring hurt too much, so that she cried in pain, and fell forward. Then, inch by inch, she began to crawl towards the back door. It was only yards away, but every move was an effort. Nearer—nearer still—only two more yards, and the steps, and she would be safe. When——

'My God, Tammy, don't try and move!' She saw Blaise in the doorway, then coming down towards her, tried to warn him about the ice, but it came out in a croak, and the next second he was kneeling down beside her, helping her up, gently, using his strength to support her, and lift her.

'I slipped—ice—near the dustbin—I couldn't——'

'Ssh! Let's get in. Don't try to talk.' He picked her up and carried her through into the lounge and laid her on the settee, then knelt beside her, rubbing her frozen hands. 'You fell near the dustbin on some ice. Right?' She nodded. 'Where does it hurt?' he asked her.

'My right leg—I haven't broken it, I don't think. I mean, I didn't hear a crack or anything, but it hurt when I tried to stand up, and I fell again——'

'All right, save your strength. I heard you shout. Don't move now. I'm going to get this fire lit and have

a look at your leg.' He vanished, to return a minute
later with the empty ash can which he put underneath
the fire before lighting it. 'Let's see. I can't give you a
drink yet in case you've busted a bone and it has to be
set, but just bear with me until I've had a good look,
okay?'

'Yes.' She lay back. He started at her foot, and she
cried out—and then looked at him as he said:

'It's your ankle. You've sprained it badly, Tammy,
and with any luck, that's all you've done. Keep your
fingers crossed.' Very gently, he felt up her leg to the
knee—and she knew he was right. The pain that had
made her fall again was centred in her right ankle.
Now that the weight was off it, there was nothing
when he touched anywhere else. Already her ankle
was puffy and white, and she closed her eyes in relief.

'That's all? You're sure?'

'I'm sure. I'll make you some strong coffee. That
and a couple of painkillers, and a good cold wet
bandage, will ease the pain a lot. Just to be sure, I'll
take you to a doctor's later.'

'I feel better already,' she managed.

'Good.' He crouched beside the settee, and he was
too close for comfort, much too close, but his manner
had none of its usual aggression. She looked into his
face, and saw only concern in his eyes, and wanted to
cry. He looked back at her, seemed about to say something, then stood up. 'I'll make the drink.' He went
out, bringing a blanket in a minute later, and laying it
over her. 'You need to keep warm.'

'Yes. Blaise, you won't wake Fiona, will you?'

'I won't. She needs her sleep. Stay still, I'll not be
long.' He left her again and she watched the paper
spills burning, catching the wood, crackling and smok-

ing, not warming the room yet, but promising to shortly. She lay back. This wasn't going to spoil anything, on that she was already decided. It might even be turned to advantage ... She wasn't sure how, just yet, but she was prepared to work on it. It could make Blaise a little less prickly, for a start, and that was no bad thing. Tamsin, when it suited her, wasn't above playing the helpless little woman—and when circumstances called for it, as well they might, she would do so without a qualm. She smiled to herself, then winced with pain as her ankle reminded her what had happened. 'Damn it,' she muttered.

'Swear if it helps.' Blaise came in carrying a steaming beaker. 'Sit up—that's it. Now take these as well,' he handed her two white pills. 'They're only paracetomol, but they'll help. It's too early to go to the doctor's—it's not an emergency—but at nine I'll take you.'

'Thank you.' She swallowed the pills and drank some coffee. 'I'm sorry I got you out of bed.' She allowed two huge tears to well up in her eyes. It was a trick she'd learnt in childhood. 'I tried to get back in the house without making a fuss——'

'And what would you have done then?' He stood looking down at her.

'Lit the cooker or gas fire—anything to keep warm, and stayed in the kitchen till someone got up.'

He pulled up a straight-backed chair and sat down. 'I believe you would have.'

'What else was there to do?'

'Yell like hell, of course.'

She shook her head. 'I didn't want to wake Fiona or the children—I wouldn't have done that.'

'You're amazing!' He sounded as if he meant it.

'Why?'

'Most women would have screamed the place down.'

She looked at him in amazement. 'How do you know? Anyway, I'm not "most" women, I'm me.'

'Yes.' He stood up. 'I'd better go and find something to bind round that foot of yours. Any ideas?'

She thought for a moment. 'There's some mutton-cloth in the glove compartment of my car. I use it for wiping the windows—it's quite clean. If you soak it, then put it in the fridge for ten minutes, that will do the trick.' There was the merest trace of a smile on his face and she frowned. 'What's the matter?'

'You. You should have been a doctor. Hang on, I'll get it.' He went out, and Tamsin left to ponder his remark. He'd not been sarcastic, merely amused. She lay back and waited—and waited.

It seemed ages before he returned, and he carried a bowl, and the dripping cloth, which he bound tightly round her ankle and secured with a pin. 'Okay? Does that feel better?'

'Much better, thanks. I'll get up soon——'

'Not until you've been to the doctor's you won't.'

'I can't go like this, can I?' she pointed out, reasonably enough.

'I don't see why not, with a coat over. You're certainly not hopping around getting dressed until we're sure nothing's broken—and while I'm pretty sure, I'm not a doctor. You understand?'

'I don't have much choice in the matter.'

'No, you don't. You can have a piece of toast if you want, and that's all. Just in case.'

'Please. Er—I promised Fiona breakfast in bed this morning——'

'I'll take it to her before we go. She'll have to be woken up before then, or she'll wonder where the hell we've gone.'

'Thanks.'

'Anything else?' he enquired dryly.

'Er—no.'

'That's a relief. I'll make your toast now.'

It was working out quite nicely. She could persuade them all to go shopping later and then phone Mario, if only to warn him to keep out of sight in case they went by his hotel, which was just outside the village where they normally shopped. She picked up her bag to write the shopping list, and the piece of paper with his telephone number fell out and fluttered to the floor just out of her reach. She stared at it in horror. If Blaise should come in ... But she could hear him whistling in the kitchen, and the clatter of plates. Easing herself off the settee, Tamsin reached out, further, then further still until her fingers touched the elusive scrap of paper—touched, but could not hold. Almost crying in frustration, she stretched that extra inch, grabbed the paper—and fell with a resounding thud to the floor. As she lay there, she had the sense to stuff the paper in her dressing gown pocket—and she heard his exclamation, running footsteps—and he burst in. 'Tammy—good God, woman, what on earth——'

'I fell,' she said unnecessarily. She was more winded than hurt.

'I can see that.' He lifted her up again. 'But what the hell were you doing?'

She could hardly tell him. It was a time for swift action. 'Oh,' she moaned, and burst into beautifully realistic tears, 'I ache all over—please don't shout——'

'Don't cry, love. I'm sorry.' His arms were around her, gentle, not hard. 'It's all right—but you shouldn't try to move——' his voice was muffled, and she clung to him, feeling his head on her breast, a delightful and treacherous warmth stealing through her. She didn't care that he only wanted to soothe her because he thought she was upset. She was filled with the heady sense of power that she knew she possessed over him at that moment. It was enough. It was more—it was quite delightful.

'I'm sorry,' she sobbed, her voice a little helpless whisper. 'I dropped my—my bag and I didn't want——' she stopped, and clutched him firmly. 'Oh—my foot—oh!'

'Sshh,' he stroked her face gently. 'Easy now, easy.'

'Don't leave me. I hurt.'

'I won't leave you.' He knelt, and held her, and his voice was gentle. Tamsin knew she was being totally and utterly irresponsible, and she didn't give a damn. She was safe, more safe than she had ever been with him, and they both knew it. She allowed herself to go limp, and she breathed in little tremulous gasps, and she was enjoying herself immensely, and she would probably think why later, and feel quite ashamed, but at that moment it didn't seem to matter. She decided that he was going to kiss her, and stirred slightly—accidentally, so that his face was very near, so close that she could see every detail of it, and she whispered:

'I'm sorry I'm being such a baby. It's reaction, I suppose—please forgive me.' It was a soft, sweet murmur to his cheek, and she moved imperceptibly forward and their faces touched and she smelt the masculine scent of him, brushed his cheek with her mouth and breathed softly, and he too moved that fraction of an inch, almost without seeming to, then his lips were on hers, and this time, now, it was very different. It was all the difference in the world, a caress, a caring, a gentleness that went on and on until time seemed to stand still, and there were only the two of them that existed. Nothing else mattered. There was only the softness of mouth on mouth, and the heady sweetness of it all, and his hand upon her neck, touching gently, not attempting anything more, stroking her as if nothing else had ever been.

Lost, timeless, all pain gone, Tamsin felt as if she were floating, in space, in a dreamtime that was endless and would go on for ever and ever and ever ... She touched his face, then his head, and she stroked his hair, and he lifted his face away, and she saw his eyes darker than she had ever seen them, half closed, then he kissed her again. He kissed her as if it was the only thing he had ever wanted to do in his life, and she almost purred with the ecstasy of it all, and it could well have gone on for ever—until, suddenly, he moved, and, voice muffled, said: 'Oh God,' then wrenched himself away from her and walked out of the room. Or did he stagger? She couldn't be sure. She heard the crash of a plate from the kitchen, and began to laugh softly to herself. Taking the scrap of paper from her pocket, she zipped it safely in the centre purse of her bag, and lay back, satisfied. She'd proved something—but she wasn't sure what it was, yet.

CHAPTER TEN

BLAISE was a troubled man. And Tamsin was enjoying herself. She sat on the settee, mid-morning, her foot up on a stool, and watched the children squabbling over a game in the corner, and waited for Fiona to bring in her cup of coffee. For something odd and completely unexpected had happened. When Blaise had taken up his sister's breakfast and told her of Tamsin's accident, she had insisted on getting up immediately, rushed into the lounge and exclaimed: 'Why didn't you wake me before?'

'Because you need your rest, and you're supposed to be here to be looked after, remember?' Tamsin had answered. Fiona's reply had been totally unforeseen.

'The hell with that! I've just realised I've been looked after for too long—and if you think I'm going to sit around while you struggle about with an injured foot you're mistaken. Oh, Tammy! You poor thing,' and she had sat beside her, and clasped Tamsin's hand, and they had both started to giggle like a couple of schoolgirls so that Blaise, coming in and seeing them, had stood there looking thunderstruck. Fiona had looked up at him and laughed out loud. 'It's all right, brother mine, I've not gone crazy—just go and get the car ready to take Tammy to the doctor's.' And when he hadn't moved, 'Go *on*! The earlier you get there the sooner you'll be back.' He had gone out, and

155

Fiona had looked at Tamsin, 'Men! Aren't they stupid at times? Now, I'll get you a coat and we'll wrap you up——'

'But,' protested Tamsin weakly, 'I don't understand. You're not——'

'Fiddlesticks! I needed something to jolt me out of my self-pitying state, and you've just done it. Don't you *see*? Everyone dashes around looking after *me*, and I've let them. Well, now I've suddenly grown up. I'll have a lovely breakfast waiting for you when you come back.' She had hugged Tamsin impulsively. 'And then *I'll* look after you—and the children—and *him*!' Her face, that soft gentle face, was transformed. She had come alive. Tamsin, bemused, had allowed her to help her on with a coat, and out to the waiting car, and a sense of rightness filled her. She still wasn't sure what had happened—but whatever it was, it was working. She was brought back to the present by the arrival of Fiona with a steaming beaker of coffee, and looked up.

'Thanks. Fiona, are you sure you're well enough——'

Fiona sat down beside her. 'I've never felt so good for years. Now, what else needs doing?'

'Well, there's lunch. We'll do that together——' and as Fiona started to speak—'Wait, I'm not sitting here all day either, you know, or I'll go mad. We'll get him out of the kitchen—let him play with the children or take them out in the garden—and we'll do something super to celebrate the new Fiona.'

'Sounds fine. All right, drink your coffee, then we'll move.'

Ten minutes later they were both sitting in the kitchen peeling onions, and crying their eyes out and laughing, all at the same time. 'I don't know why onions always have this effect on me,' sniffed Tamsin.

'Nor me,' agreed Fiona, wiping away the tears. Blaise walked in, took a swift startled look, and vanished again. They stared at each other, suppressing the laughter that threatened—then burst out, helplessly, into gales of laughter. 'Did you *see* his face?' roared Fiona.

'He must think we're mad!' gasped Tamsin.

'Wait till I tell him what he's got to go and buy. He'll *know* we're mad!'

'What's that?'

'Garlic.'

'Garlic!' exclaimed Tamsin, wide-eyed.

'My dear Tammy, you can't do a proper spaghetti without that. I'll go and shout him now,' and she did. When he came in, she said:

'Will you take the children to the village and buy some cloves of garlic—and if they don't have any go into a grocers and get a jar of garlic flakes or powder— oh! and you'd better get a couple of packets of spaghetti as well.' Blaise looked at her, expressionless.

'Anything else?'

'Well, yes, now you come to mention it, there is. We'd better make a list, hadn't we, Tammy?'

'Shout me when you've done it,' he said tersely, and left them. He didn't exactly slam the door when he went out, but it was near enough.

Fiona pulled a face. 'Oh dear, Blaise isn't very sunny today. I wonder why?'

Tamsin thought she knew, and she smiled. She sensed another reason too. 'I think he's puzzled because we get on so well—you don't think he possibly feels left out, do you?'

'Blaise—left out? As if he'd care——' Then she stopped, regarding Tamsin very thoughtfully. 'You know, you might have a point at that! Don't forget he's used to seeing me very quiet and sorry for myself. I'll bet he's puzzled more than anything. Poor Blaise!'

Poor Blaise indeed, echoed Tamsin silently. She had a growing sense of inner calm, difficult to explain, but there all the same. She began to think that her little accident was possibly the best thing that could have happened. It had certainly transformed Fiona.

'We'd better make that list,' she said. 'The sooner he goes, the better—oh, ouch!'

'What's the matter?'

'Just my foot. If I forget, and move it, it hurts like hell. The doctor said to keep it off the ground as much as possible for a day or two——'

'I'm sorry, love,' said Fiona. 'Can I get you an aspirin or anything?'

'No.' Tamsin laughed. 'Don't look so worried. I'll live.'

'I know. But it's a nuisance. Now—the list. You dictate, I'll write.'

She called Blaise when it was done and he looked at it, then at them. 'I'll go now with the kids,' he said.

'Yes, and be as quick as you can,' said Fiona.

'I don't have the helicopter here, or I'd take that,' he answered coolly. 'However, I'll be as quick as possible, speed limits permitting.'

'Yes, you do that,' retorted Fiona cheerfully. 'And —oh yes, get a bottle of wine if you see an off-licence open. We might as well lunch in style.'

'Sure you don't want champagne?'

'Wine will do.' She smiled sweetly at him. 'And

keep the car window open. The fresh air might improve your temper.'

'There's nothing wrong with it, thanks.'

'Isn't there? You've been like a bear with a sore head all morning.' Tamsin sat quietly dicing up the onions and assuming an air of polite indifference, as though she couldn't hear a thing. She dared not look at Fiona for fear of laughing. Instead she concentrated on her task.

'Perhaps it's because I'm expected to act as nurse-maid while you two giggle the morning away,' he answered.

'You can leave the children here—or would you prefer me to go to the village?' Fiona stood up. 'I'll go, then you can get on with your precious writing. Give me the list.' She snatched it from him.

'Don't be stupid. You don't know your way around.' He took it back from her.

Tamsin found herself rather weary of it all. She was annoyed with Blaise. 'I'll go with Fiona and show her the way,' she said. He turned on her.

'Why don't you keep out of this? It's nothing to do with you.'

'Don't you speak to Tammy like that!' snapped Fiona.

'It's all right, I'm used to it,' Tamsin answered. She glared at Blaise standing there stony-faced. 'Fiona and I will go—and we'll take the children.' She stood up, fumbling for the walking stick they had found.

'Don't be so bloody martyred. I'm going now.' And he walked out, slamming the door. Fiona and Tamsin sat down and looked at one another.

'Well!' said Fiona. 'I could cheerfully have hit him.

I don't think I've had a row with Blaise since we were children. Just wait till I get him alone after lunch!'

'I wouldn't bother,' said Tamsin. 'The best thing to do is ignore it. You'll see, he'll have cooled down when he gets back.'

'He'd better.' Fiona scooped the prepared onions into a pan, and put it on the stove. 'We'll see anyway.'

Tamsin was right. When Blaise returned half an hour later, the aggression appeared to have gone. He brought in the box of provisions and put them on the table, then went out without a word. Silently, Fiona picked up the litre bottle of rosé wine, opened it, and poured out two glasses. 'We need this,' she said. 'Cheers.'

'Cheers.'

The bottle was nearly empty by the time lunch was ready, and they were past caring. Tamsin found that it had the most pleasant effect on her; the pain in her ankle was completely forgotten and her cheeks were flushed. She looked across the kitchen at Fiona, busily stirring at the stove. 'I feel all rosy,' she said.

'Rosy—rosé! I like that.' Fiona began to giggle helplessly. Blaise chose that unfortunate moment to walk in. He took a look at the bottle on the table, then at them.

'Have some,' said Tamsin.

'There's hardly any left,' he answered. 'But if it's done you two good, what does it matter?'

'True,' hiccupped Fiona. 'Very true. Sit down, Blaise, lunch is nearly ready.'

'I'll get the kids in.' He was *furious*, that was quite obvious. The awful thing was that it set them off laughing again. They tried to sober up for his return with Peter and Paula, but the more they tried the worse they became. With shaking shoulders and streaming eyes, Fiona attempted to ladle spaghetti on to each plate with disastrous results, watched by the helpless Tamsin. Blaise came in, took one look at his sister, and marched over to her, taking the pan out of her hands. 'Sit *down*,' he said. 'I'll do it.'

Peter and Paula watched with interest as the last of the large bottle was poured out. 'Can we have some, Mummy?' asked the spokeswoman.

'Just a little, dears—with water. That's it. Tammy, you've done the cheese, haven't you?'

'Mmm—whoops!' It reached the table safely—just, and they began to eat. It was delicious, no doubt about that, and because the children were present, the meal passed without incident. When the last morsels had vanished from the plates, and all was cleared away, Blaise stood up.

'I'll take the kids out for the afternoon,' he said, 'and this evening I shall be writing in here, so I would appreciate if it's all straight for me to work in after about six o'clock.' He smiled pleasantly at them both—presumably for the children's benefit—and added: 'Is that clear?'

Fiona gave him a dreamy smile. 'Quite so.' She waited until the three of them had gone out of the room. 'Phew!' she said. 'I don't think he likes us very much at the moment.'

'He doesn't like me at all,' said Tamsin dryly. 'I'm *tired*.'

'So'm I. Let's clear away, then go and sit in the lounge with a coffee.'

'Lovely idea.' They worked well and quickly, and prepared a salad, which they put in the refrigerator. Then they took a pot of coffee and two cups into the lounge, settled down by the fire, talked for a while—and both fell asleep.

Blaise woke them up when he came in, took one look at the puzzled, half-asleep expressions of his sister and Tamsin, said: 'My God!' with some feeling, then went out, slamming the door.

Shamefaced, they looked at one another. 'Oh, my head,' moaned Fiona. 'I've never done that before.'

'Nor me,' confessed Tamsin. 'That's it. I think we'd better stay sober in future.'

'Agreed.' They shook hands solemnly on it.

'You know,' said Fiona, 'we've been awful to Blaise today. And he's very good, really.'

'I suppose he is.'

'He offered to bring them away, so I could rest—and what have I done? Treated him like an errand boy——'

'Or a nursemaid.'

'Or, indeed, as a nursemaid, as you say. I'm a rotten sister.'

'No, you're not.'

'Yes, I am. Let's go and be nice to him.'

'Do we *have* to? asked Tamsin in faint alarm.

They both burst out laughing. 'Yes. Come on, we'll make him a nice cup of coffee.'

They went out to the kitchen, Tamsin slower and walking more carefully, and Blaise was looking around for food.

'We've come to make you a coffee,' announced Fiona. 'Go and sit down.'

He looked sourly at them. 'I've sent the kids out to make a snowman,' he said. 'I was going to get tea ready.'

'But it's done! We've agreed that you're too good

for words, and now we're going to look after you.
Aren't we, Tammy?'

'Yes.'

'That should be a pleasant change. I'll believe it
when I see it.'

He looked at Tamsin, and she saw that in his eyes
that she had seen before, and she went warm inside.
Warm and confused. 'I'll put the kettle on,' she said,
then saw that it already was. 'Oh!'

'I think I'll go and play with my children,' said
Fiona, and grabbed Blaise's jacket from a chair, put it
on, and went out. Tamsin and Blaise were alone. She
took a deep breath.

'Sober?' he enquired.

'I wasn't drunk.'

'You could have fooled me.'

'I'm not going to argue with you,' she answered.
'You heard what your sister said, so if you want to
insult me, go ahead.'

'I wouldn't know where to begin.'

'That'll make a change, won't it?' She put coffee in
three cups.

'*You* haven't changed, anyway.'

She stared at him. 'And what does that mean?'

'Fiona has, since she came here. Whether it's for the
better is too early to say.'

'Well, she seems all right to me.'

'She would, though. You're like two giggly bosom
pals.'

'Perhaps that's what she's been short of, a bit of
laughter.'

'Perhaps.' He shrugged. 'I wouldn't know.'

'That's your trouble. You're too busy with your
nose buried in a typewriter to bother about people.'

'I thought you weren't going to argue.'

'I changed my mind. You'd make a parson swear.'

'Can't you be more original than that?'

She rounded on him. 'No, damn you, I can't! Not possessing your literary gifts I have to express myself like ordinary people do——'

'You're not ordinary. You're a little scheming spitfire with a temper like——'

'Oh, shut up!' Her eyes blazed. 'Go and watch the television or something. I don't want to talk to *you*.' She poured boiling water into a beaker. 'And take your damned coffee with you!'

'If that's what you call looking after me I'd rather look after myself.'

'And that's what I'd prefer you to do. You're an arrogant, impossible, argumentative *beast*——'

'And you can thank your lucky stars you've a sprained ankle. *And* that you're a woman——'

'Oh, you had noticed?' She laughed. 'There's hope for you yet. Yes, of course you had. I'd forgotten your attempted rape the other night.' She looked him up and down. 'But then it was hardly worth remembering.'

She saw his face change. She had gone too far, and she knew it.

'Perhaps the next time will be more memorable,' he said. 'I'll make sure of it.'

'You won't get the chance,' she retorted.

'Don't be too sure. It would hardly have been rape.' He smiled in a way that sent a shiver through her. 'Would it? If the kids hadn't cried out——'

'Get out of here.' She was trembling with rage. 'Get *out*!'

'When I'm ready. Touched a nerve, did I?' He

moved over nearer to her. 'You were all ready to find out what it was all about, weren't you? And you didn't. Shame! Didn't Nigel ever teach you?'

She swung wildly at him, missed, and nearly fell, but he caught her. 'Careful. Well, well, he didn't.'

'Let me *go*!'

'You said that somewhere before.'

She hit him in the stomach, and winced at the hardness of his muscles.

'I'm stronger than you think. You might do well to remember that.' And as he released her, he deliberately ran his hand down her body. 'Far tougher than you are, Miss Tammy.' His hand burned where it had touched, and she was helpless to retaliate. He took his beaker, gave her a long, lingering look, and smiled. 'You've got a figure like a boy.' He laughed. 'No wonder you can't get a man.' And he walked out of the kitchen.

Tamsin wanted to run after him, but she couldn't. 'I hate you. I *hate* you!' she cried, and stared at the closed door. Then she put her hand to her mouth, biting her knuckles, wanting to scream.

Fiona popped her head round the outer door. 'Were you having a fight?' she whispered. 'I heard raised voices.'

'I could *kill* him!' whispered Tamsin.

'Oh *dear*.' Fiona came in and closed the door after her. 'I shouldn't have gone out, should I?'

'He's—he's—*impossible*!'

Fiona sighed. 'They all are, love. Where's he gone?'

'I don't know. I don't care if I never see him again!'

'You have got it bad, haven't you?' observed Fiona.

Tamsin stared at her. 'What—what do you mean?'

'Fighting like that. It's a bad sign. It usually leads to——' she lowered her voice, '*other things.*'

'Huh! Not with him it doesn't. He won't get the chance.'

'Hmm. I'd watch him if I were you.'

'Why do you think I moved in with the children?' Fiona's eyes widened. 'You mean——'

'I'll tell you some other time. Not now.'

Fiona started to laugh. 'I don't believe it. He must be human after all. No wonder you wanted me here!'

Suddenly it seemed the time. 'There was another reason—as well,' said Tamsin slowly.

Fiona looked at her slowly, very slowly, and very unsure of herself. She shook her head. 'No,' she said.

'No what?'

'It can't be—no.'

'It can't be—what?'

Fiona shrugged. 'Is the coffee ready? Oh, nothing. I just had the most ridiculous idea——'

'Then say it.'

'I can't. You'd laugh.'

'I might not. Try me.'

'All right.' She stared at Tamsin. 'Have you—er— *seen* anyone since you've been here?'

'Yes,' said Tamsin, and waited.

'Dear God,' murmured Fiona. 'Was it—a man?'

'Yes.'

'Was it——' she looked at Tamsin, and there was all the world in her eyes, and she was suddenly small, and afraid, and vulnerable, so that Tamsin, unable to bear her agony any longer, said softly:

'It was your husband. He loves you more than his life. And he loves the children—and that's why I persuaded you to come.'

Fiona sat in a chair as though all the strength had been knocked from her. 'I'm dreaming,' she said. 'Please help me.'

'No, you're not.' Tamsin walked, with difficulty, over to her, and sat in the chair beside her. 'Please forgive me, Fiona. I saw him, and we talked, and I knew——' She stopped.

'You knew——?'

'I knew that it was all wrong—that I had to help. So I phoned you——' she burst into tears of sheer relief at having, at last, been able to speak.

'Oh, Tammy, don't! Don't cry. *I'm* not—look at me. Just please—*please* tell me.' Fiona was trembling.

So Tamsin, slowly and carefully, remembering, told her. She began at the very beginning, with the walk in the snow with the children, and seeing the car drawing nearer, and as she spoke, she was there again, and because it was so vivid and real to her, the words came freely, and the tears died away, and as she went on, quietly and with heartfelt sincerity, she saw that Fiona was there too, sharing the scenes, hearing the words, knowing, at last, the truth.

When she had finished, there was silence. 'I—knew—I've known, sisce I came here——' Fiona paused.

Tamsin looked at her. 'Known what?'

'That there was something. Something about this place.' She caught hold of Tamsin's hand. 'But I didn't know what. Only the feeling——' she looked around the room. 'I don't *know*, but you——'

'Well, don't stop there. What about me?' Tamsin demanded in mock severity.

'It was as if you knew something. And as soon as I met you, I trusted you—as though I'd known you all my life. And I'm a very reserved person usually. But I felt like—like—coming home.'

Tamsin gave a deep sigh. 'Ah, now I know what you mean. It's all right.'

'Where is he?'

'Not six miles from here, in a hotel. I said I'd call him, when I had any news for him.'

'Then call him now.'

'But——'

'Please! Now.'

'Don't you want to think about what I've told you?'

'I've had a lot of time to think, Tammy. I've had all the time in the world. Please phone him—and then let me talk to him.'

Tamsin stood up. 'Come on, then. We'll do it now, before tea. And tonight—perhaps——'

Fiona actually blushed. 'I want to see him, and talk to him, but I think it's better Blaise doesn't know. Not yet. Not until——'

'I know. Let's think a moment. He's watching television, at least I think he is. We don't want him to hear.' They sat in a lovely, companionable silence for a minute or two, and thought about it.

'Got it!' Tamsin snapped her fingers.

'Yes?'

'Let's have tea. It's ready, don't forget, apart from opening that tin of ham, and then we'll shove them all in the lounge because there's a John Wayne film on——'

'And Blaise likes a good Western——'

'Yes, precisely. *Then* we'll phone, and take it from there.'

'Yes. Oh yes!' Fiona's eyes shone. Tamsin sat down.

'Pass me the ham. And call 'em in.'

'Right.'

Ten minutes later they were all eating. Both Fiona and Tamsin were stone cold sober, but filled with an excitement, a planning, that coloured their every action. Tamsin felt almost sorry for Blaise. He looked like a man who didn't know what was happening, only that he was excluded—and knew it. Even the children were aware of something odd in the atmosphere, and they looked from their mother to Tamsin, and back again—and exchanged glances, pulling faces until Fiona rebuked them firmly. 'Eat up, you two,' she said, 'and behave.' Then she looked at Tamsin and her mouth twitched.

'More ham, Blaise?' Tamsin enquired.

'No, thanks, I've had enough.' He had changed. He was icily polite. She sighed. Some people there was just no pleasing, she thought contentedly. But she didn't really care. Everything else was working out beautifully. Her father would be pleased when he knew.

The minutes seemed to drag their feet. But eventually all was ready—until Blaise said, in surprise, that he had no intention of watching any television. He was going to write—or had they forgotten? They had.

Tamsin signalled to Fiona not to worry. If the telephone was difficult there was another, simpler and far more direct method of communication. It needed only a little more patience. She explained it to Fiona as they washed the dishes. 'We'll go to the hotel,' she said. 'Saves phoning. We'll just go. Then I'll leave you talking and come home here.'

'But you can't drive,' Fiona whispered back. Tamsin hadn't thought of that one.

'I'll get a taxi. Mario can guide you back here——'

'Are you sure?'

'*Yes*. Ssh!' This as Blaise came in and began getting out his typewriter and paper in a very decisive manner.

'Then we'll wait until the children are in bed——' Fiona barely mouthed the words, and Tamsin nodded.

'I'll give the children a bath,' Fiona said out loud.

'That's a good idea. I'll help you.'

'Then we'll watch television, and let Blaise get on with his play——'

'Oh yes, we must.' They nudged each other silently.

'Your concern is most touching,' he said.

'Isn't it?' agreed his sister. She looked at Tamsin, and winked. 'Mind you, I wouldn't mind going out for a little drink.'

'Now *that's* a good idea too. It will do us both good.'

'You'd get stopped for drunken driving,' was his acid comment.

'Don't be stuffy! I'll be driving—and I won't have more than one,' retorted Fiona.

'Don't be stupid.'

Fiona pulled a face at Tamsin. 'Are you telling me I can't go?'

'You're old enough to decide for yourself. I'm not your keeper.'

'Right, then.' She flung the tea towel to one side. 'That's decided. Blaise can babysit while we have an hour or two out. Come on, let's run the bathwater and get the children to bed. An early night won't hurt them. The kitchen is all yours, Blaise. Happy typing!'

Tamsin glanced back as they went out. She saw a very puzzled man, watching her. She smiled and gave him a pretty wave. 'All yours,' she repeated. She wished that she could tell him. But he would know, soon enough. Then she would be able to leave. And she would never see him again, she knew that. It couldn't be soon enough.

She followed Fiona out, and closed the door behind her. She only wished that she could stop loving him as easily.

CHAPTER ELEVEN

THE hotel loomed up, lights blazing, several hundred yards ahead.

'I'm scared,' said Fiona. 'I feel sick.'

'No, you don't,' responded Tamsin sharply. 'You feel fine.'

'I feel fine,' echoed Fiona, unconvinced.

'And you look lovely.'

'I look—no, I don't—oh, Tammy, stay with me.'

'Of course I will,' Tamsin answered soothingly.

'Promise?'

'Promise.'

Fiona swung into the hotel car park and found a parking space. 'What if he's not there?'

'He will be.'

'I feel like a girl on my first date.'

'That's nice. Just pretend you are.'

'You *know* what I mean. Oh, Tammy, please don't leave——'

'If you say that again, I will,' Tamsin threatened. 'So shut up, and help me in.'

'Yes, Tammy. What would I do without you?'

'You'd still be at home in Stirling feeling sorry for yourself. Right?'

'Right. Here we go. Deep breath—and away.'

They walked into the reception hall slowly, and went over to the desk. 'Mr Zandradi, please,' said

Tamsin, cool, calm and collected, because someone had to be, and it wasn't going to be Fiona, that was sure.

'Yes, madame, I think he's dining. One moment, please.' For a small country hotel, it was efficiently run, and Tamsin looked round appreciatively. What a nice place to have a meal with a man you loved! She put the thought out of her mind.

Then she saw him. She saw him first, because Fiona was fiddling with her handbag mirror, doing a last-minute nervous check, and Tamsin saw the look on his face as he walked towards them from the dining room, and she touched Fiona's arm.

'I think you'd better look up,' she said quietly.

She would never forget what happened then for as long as she lived. She saw them both, and she might not have been there at all. She saw their faces. The tremulous, frightened look on Fiona's, the gentle, all encompassing love shining out from Mario's as he walked up, took Fiona's hand, and said, very softly: 'Fiona.' The word was a caress. It sent shivers up Tamsin's spine. She swallowed hard. If a man ever loved me like that, she thought, I'd die happily.

They were looking at each other as if the world was a wonderful place they'd just discovered—and only they were in it.

'I'll just have to go and powder my nose,' said Tamsin. She didn't know if they had heard her. They didn't appear to have done. 'If you'll excuse me,' she added, and she went.

She composed herself, waited five minutes, then went out again. They had gone. Then she saw them, sitting talking on a long settee outside the lounge, and walked over.

Mario jumped to his feet. 'Tammy, forgive me,' he said, and kissed her on both cheeks. 'How can I thank you?'

She sat down. 'I don't think you need to.' She looked at her watch. 'Heavens, is that the time? Doesn't it fly?'

Fiona began to laugh. 'Tammy, you idiot! We're going to have a drink, and a talk, in Mario's room. He's ordered champagne. There's a lift——'

'No,' said Tamsin.

'But you promised!'

She looked at them both. '*That* was then. You don't need me now. Do you?'

She caught the look they exchanged. They definitely didn't need anyone. She sighed a gentle sigh. 'Just let's have one drink down here, then I'll order a taxi and go home.'

Mario stood up. 'I will get them. Please stay, Tammy, for a while at least. We owe you so much——'

'You owe me nothing, Mario, neither of you. My reward is just seeing you together. And the rest is up to you.' She smiled. 'All right, one drink. A dry Martini—and will you book a taxi for—say—fifteen minutes?'

He nodded and left them. Fiona looked at Tamsin. 'I love him,' she said simply.

'I know. That's why I'm going. You don't need me here, you have to talk, to sort things out, and that's best done alone. I knew this would happen, and I can't tell you how happy I am.' She pressed Fiona's hand. 'Don't you see? It's what I planned when I first saw him.'

'You're a witch!' exclaimed Fiona.

'Perhaps. I wish I was. I wouldn't need a taxi then, would I? Just my broomstick!'

They were still laughing when Mario returned, so they had to tell him the joke, and he joined in their laughter, but it was obvious, to Tamsin at least, that he was eager to have his wife on her own. She didn't know why she should suddenly feel sad. This was what she had wanted all along, and it had worked out like a dream, just perfectly, and she should be feeling very pleased with herself—and she was, in a way, but in another way she felt a strange sense of desolation.

On the way home, some twenty minutes later, she realized why. The kitchen light was on, and the sound of typing came clearly down the hall as she let herself in. Blaise had left the kitchen door open, presumably to listen out for the children in case they woke. She leaned against the front door for a moment, her foot hurting, hearing the taxi drive away until that sound vanished. Then she began to walk towards the kitchen.

'I'm back,' she said. He barely looked up and she wasn't sure if he grasped the significance of the 'I'. 'Coffee?'

'If you're making it.'

'I am.' She busied herself at the stove, made two cups of coffee, and handed him one.

As she went out, he looked up. 'Where's Fiona?'

'She'll be back later.' She closed the door, went into the lounge, and waited. She had only counted to twenty by the time he came in.

'What do you mean—later?' He didn't look angry. He didn't look anything particularly, only like a man who's not sure if he's heard correctly.

Tamsin, who had been feeling reasonably composed

up until that moment, suddenly found herself filled with an unreasoning panic. She stared at him. 'What?'

'I said—what do you mean, later? Is she here or not? And if she's not, where the hell is she? You didn't *forget* her, did you?'

'No. She's having a drink—she met someone.' He stared at her, his face dark with anger.

'She picked someone up, you mean?'

'I think you'd better s-sit down.'

'I'll stand. What goes on here? I know you're bloody mad, but I didn't think she was—not until she met you, anyway——'

'I'm not even bothering to listen to you if you're going to stand there ranting and raving,' Tamsin retorted, her panic disappearing in the face of the sudden flare of his rage.

He walked over and jerked her to her feet and shook her. 'You'll damn well listen to me whether you like it or not,' he said harshly.

'You're hurting me!' She went white with the shock of his assault, and with the sudden blaze of pain from her jolted ankle. 'Please——'

He released her, towering over her. 'All right——' she gasped. 'I'll tell you—but you might not like it—and I don't care. She's with Mario.'

'For God's sake!' She thought, for a second, that he was going to knock her down, but she stood her ground. 'Mario? *Mario*—it's impossible!'

'Is it? Then don't bother to ask me if you're not going to believe me.'

'It was him you met the other night, wasn't it?' his voice shook with the violence that gripped him.

'Yes. Yes, it was—and I arranged it all—that's why I persuaded her to come down here—and there's nothing you can do about it, because—she loves him, and he loves her——'

'She's sick—she's not in a fit state to decide—where are they?'

'She's as fit as you or I—and she's well able to make her own mind up. She's an adult, or had you forgotten? You seem to think——'

'I'm not concerned in your opinions. Where are they?'

'I've no intention of telling you!'

'Then I can guess. I'll phone all the hotels round here until I find out——' He shook her arm as she tried to restrain him, and stalked out, face like thunder.

He was picking up the telephone when she reached him. 'Don't,' she begged. 'Please—just listen to me first.' He looked at her.

'Why should I? You've done enough damage already. The man's dangerous—he kidnapped his children and took them off——'

'No! I know the truth. I've heard both sides—which is more than you have, I know. Please, please, just let me tell you—and then, if you still feel the same way, I'll tell you where they are.'

It was a gamble, she knew that. But she also knew that in his present dangerous mood, anything could happen. She stood there, swaying slightly with sheer exhaustion brought about by the violence of his reaction, white-faced, desperate, and Blaise slowly put the receiver back on its rest.

'Go on.'

'Come in the lounge. I don't want to wake the children.' He followed her in and closed the door. Tamsin turned to face him, and remained standing.

She uttered a brief, silent prayer, then said: 'It happened when I took the children out for a walk in the snow a few days ago ...'

Her fear, her concern for Fiona and Mario and the two children, gave her words the force and power she needed, and by the time she was half way through the whole truthful story, with nothing left out, she sensed the imperceptible change in his mood. Only subtle, a lessening of the violent tension that held them, but it was sufficient. She reached out to hold on to a chair back, to support herself, for her foot ached intolerably, but she didn't want to sit down.

The words poured out, and her confidence grew, and she came to the scene where, in the kitchen, she had told Fiona the truth, and the tears came at the memories, but she was unaware of them, and she went on, until, at last, she had finished. She was completely drained of strength, but she found the energy to say: 'And that's it. Do you believe me——' when she felt the room tilt alarmingly, her head spinning, everything going grey and blurred, and she held on to the chair desperately, and Blaise's voice seemed to come from a long way away.

'Yes, I believe you.'

She put her hands to her head, to stop the appalling rushing sound, and heard, oh, so distantly now: 'Tammy——' just that one word before she fell, and everything was blotted out.

She opened her eyes to see him bending over her. Cold water trickled down her forehead, into her eyes, and she gasped and tried to sit up, because she didn't know what had happened.

'Stay still. You fainted.'

'I've never fainted——' the words came out as a croak.

'You just did. It's all right. Relax. You're quite safe.'

'No.' She pushed his hand away, and the cold damp facecloth fell to the carpet. 'You mustn't go——'

'I'm not going anywhere.'

She gave a deep, shuddering sigh. 'I don't want either of them—hurt.'

'I'm not going to hurt anybody. Do you want to sit up now?'

'Yes.' He lifted her as though she were a child. Just then the telephone shrilled from the hall. 'Oh——' alarm flared.

'I'll get it.' He began to walk out.

'No. It might be——'

'It's *all right*.' He went out. Tamsin heard him answer, heard him talking, and it was obvious who it was. She listened to what he was saying, heard: 'She told me everything just now. Yes—yes—no—very well—of course——' then the final words, more quietly spoken so that she could not be sure if she had heard them correctly or not: 'Fiona love, good luck.' The receiver was replaced. He walked back in and she saw in his face what she had hoped to see, and relaxed.

'She'll be back here tomorrow. They both will.' He looked at Tamsin. There was a long pause.

'I think I'll go to bed,' she said.

'Are you sure you're all right?'

'Quite sure.' She allowed him to help her to her feet. She didn't want to speak to him, because she had nothing more to say. Tomorrow she was going to go home. There was no need for her to stay. In a way she could never have foreseen, her task was completed.

'Goodnight.' She barely paused in the doorway as she said it. She didn't care if Blaise answered or not. But as she closed the door behind her, she heard his reply.

'Oh, Tammy love, you *can't* leave!' Fiona wailed. 'I won't let you——'

'You can't stop me,' was Tamsin's flippant retort. 'And anyway, you hardly need *me* now.' They were sitting in the children's bedroom the following morning. Mario was downstairs talking to his children in the lounge, Blaise had gone out in his car without saying where, and Tamsin was packing.

'But your ankle——'

'I know I can't drive, but there's a train service. I've been on the phone this morning and if you or Mario could drive me to York——'

'Please think about it,' begged Fiona.

'You know why I must go. I can't stay—not—it's Blaise,' Tamsin finished, in an incoherent burst.

'Listen, he and Mario had quite a pleasant chat after we arrived——'

'Good. That's fine. It's me he hates. I just have to get away.'

Fiona looked at Tamsin. 'I don't think he does.'

'You'd have thought so if you'd seen him last night, when I got back.'

'But he was *fine* on the phone.'

'That was after I'd told him everything. It left me feeling ill—I just had to go up to bed after, I felt as weak as a kitten.' She rubbed her ankle gently. 'Ouch, it doesn't half hurt sometimes.'

'You can't go—stay just a day or so longer——'

'No. My mind's made up. Fiona, I don't want to lose touch with you——'

'Heaven forbid! I've no intention of letting that happen, ever. We'll write, of course. I owe everything to you and I'll never forget it. I just wish I could knock some sense into that brother of mine.'

'Well, you can't. He is what he is. You swear you won't say anything when he comes back? I just want to leave with no fuss.'

'But he'll see your cases——'

'Not if we get them in Mario's car now. That's why I'm packing.'

Fiona sighed. 'You're an obstinate creature.'

'I know.'

'We'll bring your car back as soon as possible, drive it to your home, I mean. Once we've got ourselves sorted out.'

'Would you? You're a pet! I was going to suggest leaving it here and getting someone to come up in a week or so. I just want to get *home*, that's all. I might be able to think straight if I do.'

Fiona hugged her. 'You're smashing! I wish I'd got a sister like you. I've got two brothers, and lots of aunts and uncles, and my mum, of course, but I can't talk to any of them like I can to you. And now Mario's back, I can talk to him like I've never been able to before. And everything's marvellous. I can't tell you——'

'You don't need to—I can see it in your face.' Tamsin smiled. 'My father's going to get a surprise. I didn't exactly come here for matchmaking purposes, but it seems to be what I've done.'

'Tammy, when we—that is, Mario and the children and I, go back to Italy to live—will you come for a holiday?'

'I'd love to.'

'Next spring perhaps? We'd have a grand time, and Mario's got several brothers—all fair like him. A lot of northern Italians are, you know, and they're very charming——'

'Fiona, you wouldn't be trying to do some yourself, would you?'

'What?'

'Matchmaking.'

'Who, *me*?'

'Yes, you.'

'The thought never crossed my mind.'

'Hmm, I'd believe that if I couldn't see that light in your eyes.' Tamsin slammed the lid on her case. 'That's it. All done.'

'We'll take them down. Unless I can persuade you——'

'No.' She shook her head. 'You can't. Sorry.'

Three hours later she was ready to leave. Blaise was typing in the kitchen. Tamsin's cases were safely in Mario's car, and they were having their last drink together. There was a tightness in Tamsin's throat, and a prickling sensation at the back of her eyes, and it was an effort to smile, but she was doing very well. She looked at her watch. 'I don't want to miss my train,' she said. 'Could we——'

'Of course.' Mario jumped up from his chair. 'I'm ready.'

Tamsin said goodbye to Fiona and kissed the children. Then she went out, very quietly, into the

hall. For a moment she hesitated, then, to Fiona said:
'Will you say goodbye to Blaise for me?'

'I will.'

Five minutes later she was speeding down the road
with Mario. She knew she had been childish to leave
without a word to Blaise—but she didn't trust herself
to speak to him. Everything had happened so quickly.
She felt as if she wanted to sleep for at least two days—
and when she woke up, it would be time to think. It was
as if a whole lifetime had been compressed into the
period of a week—hardly more—and the mixture was
too rich. She desperately needed to be alone. Mario, as
if sensing her mood, spoke little, until, as they neared
York, he said: 'We are nearly there, Tammy.'

'I know. Please don't wait with me. I hate farewells
at stations. Just leave me outside.'

'Not with those cases. I will at least see you on to
the platform. Okay?'

'Okay.'

'And Tammy, thank you. Thank you with all my
heart. I shall never forget your kindness and your help
when I so desperately needed it.'

'Please, Mario, you're making me cry.' She began to
laugh as well, through the tears. 'I shall feel such a
fool getting on the train——' she sniffed. 'Oh dear!'

'I do not think you will be getting on the train.'
There came, at that instant, the blaring of a horn as a
car swept past, and she felt Mario slowing down.

'What? I don't understand—Mario, why have you
stopped—oh! No!' Then she knew as she saw Blaise
getting out of his car in front of theirs, and walking
towards them. 'Mario, drive——' that was as far as
she got before the door was wrenched open, and
Blaise leaned in.

'Do we talk here?' he asked. 'Or do you get in my car?'

'I'm going to catch a train,' said Tamsin. 'Do you mind?'

'No, you're not, and yes, I mind.' He looked across at the faintly smiling Mario. 'You can drive home if you like,' he said. 'Tammy and I will be a little while.'

'We won't. I'm not——'

Blaise reached in and lifted her out on to the pavement. A small queue at the bus stop across the road watched with interest. He looked at them, leaned in and said something to Mario, then slammed the door shut.

'How dare you! Open that door at——'

'I can either carry you to my car, or you can walk. Whatever you do will be observed by that fascinated little crowd over the road, and I don't really give a damn either way.'

She heard the throb of Mario's car engine, and the next moment he had gone—with her cases. It left Tamsin feeling particularly vulnerable, especially when she glanced over the road to see—and almost hear—the speculation concerning them.

'I'll walk,' she said in a dignified manner. 'But only because I have no wish to stand here brawling with you on a pavement in full view of a nosey crowd.'

'Oh, there'll be no brawling, I promise you. There'll be no nonsense from you either. I've had all I'm going to take of that from you.'

Tamsin stuck her head up high and began to walk to Blaise's car. He opened the door, and she got in. Then he walked round, gave a cheerful salute to the gaping knot of spectators and slid into the driving seat, beside her.

'Right,' he said. 'Where to?'

'York station.'

'Anywhere but there, that is.'

She glared stonily at him. 'Why have you come after me? To make me look a fool?'

'No, to talk.' He started the engine, waited for a lorry to pass, and moved swiftly into the traffic.

'I've nothing to say to you.'

'Maybe not, but I've plenty to say to you. And I'm going to find somewhere quiet to do it.'

She didn't answer him. She looked out of the window instead. They left the city, and Blaise drove down a quiet road where the houses were set well back from the road, and there was no traffic, and there he stopped.

'Now,' he said. 'Now we can talk.'

'Talk away. I won't listen. I don't want to hear anything you've got to say.'

'Then will you take notice of this?' he asked, and pulled her into his arms. Then he kissed her. She struggled momentarily, an instinctive reaction, then she stopped struggling and put her arms round him. And that was as it should be.

'Mmm,' he lifted his face slightly away, and grinned at her. 'That's better.' And she saw in his eyes what she had seen before, and now she knew what it was. She saw love. 'You know, don't you?' he said softly.

'Know what?'

'That I love you.'

'You hate me——'

'It's a strange mixture, love. It hits you hard, and it hurts sometimes—and it hit me harder, when I realised. So I reacted—I fought back, and that's just what you were doing as well, weren't you?'

'I don't know what I was doing. I'm just so confused, Blaise—I had to get away——'

'No, not from me. You'll never do that. My God, if
you knew the effect you had on me. I've hardly slept
these last few nights——'

'I wonder why?'

He buried his face in her hair. His voice was
muffled. 'You already know.'

'Tell me——' He effectively silenced her with his
mouth, and after a few minutes said huskily:

'I don't need to tell you. Don't you ever leave me
again. Don't frighten me.'

'How did you know I'd gone?' she asked.

'Paula came out crying. I asked her why—and she
told me. So I just got in my car and came after you.
Now we're going back. We'll leave tomorrow—only
we'll leave together, and I'm going to take you back
home, and meet your father and ask him for his per-
mission to ask you for your hand in marriage.'

'Really? You're just an old-fashioned boy at heart,
aren't you? Hadn't you better ask *me* first?'

'No. It's manners to wait. Besides, you might say
no. I'd like him on my side first.'

'Try me.'

'Will you? Marry me, I mean?'

'Yes.'

'When? Next week?'

She laughed. 'Only if Paula can be a bridesmaid.
You remember her asking?'

'Then she shall be. Those kids are brighter than I
thought. They'd got us all organised the minute we
met. We should have listened to them—it would have
saved us a lot of wasted time.' He switched on the
engine. 'Come on, love, let's go.' He reached out to

stroke her hair. 'Oh, I *love* you, Tammy Douglas.'

'And I love you, Blaise Torran. Oh no—Tammy Torran, can you imagine?' Laughing, they set off to drive back to the cottage and to tell the others—as if they needed telling.

In 1976 we introduced the first 100 Harlequin Collections—a selection of titles chosen from our best sellers of the past 20 years. This series, a trip down memory lane, proved how great romantic fiction can be timeless and appealing from generation to generation. The theme of love and romance is eternal, and, when placed in the hands of talented, creative, authors whose true gift lies in their ability to write from the heart, the stories reach a special level of brilliance that the passage of time cannot dim. Like a treasured heirloom, an antique of superb craftsmanship, a beautiful gift from someone loved—these stories too, have a special significance that transcends the ordinary. **$1.25 each novel**

Here are your 1978
Harlequin Collection Editions...

Original Harlequin Romance numbers in brackets

ORDER FORM
Harlequin Reader Service

In U.S.A.
MPO Box 707
Niagara Falls, N.Y. 14302

In Canada
649 Ontario St.,
Stratford, Ontario, N5A 6W2

Please send me the following Harlequin Collection novels. I am enclosing my check or money order for $1.25 for each novel ordered, plus 25¢ to cover postage and handling.

☐ 102	☐ 115	☐ 128	☐ 140
☐ 103	☐ 116	☐ 129	☐ 141
☐ 104	☐ 117	☐ 130	☐ 142
☐ 105	☐ 118	☐ 131	☐ 143
☐ 106	☐ 119	☐ 132	☐ 144
☐ 107	☐ 120	☐ 133	☐ 145
☐ 108	☐ 121	☐ 134	☐ 146
☐ 109	☐ 122	☐ 135	☐ 147
☐ 110	☐ 123	☐ 136	☐ 148
☐ 111	☐ 124	☐ 137	☐ 149
☐ 112	☐ 125	☐ 138	☐ 150
☐ 113	☐ 126	☐ 139	☐ 151
☐ 114	☐ 127		

Number of novels checked @
$1.25 each = $ _____

N.Y. and N.J. residents add
appropriate sales tax $ _____

Postage and handling $ _____.25

TOTAL $ _____

NAME _____
(Please Print)

ADDRESS _____

CITY _____

STATE/PROV. _____

ZIP/POSTAL CODE _____

A ROM 2221

Offer expires December 31, 1978

And there's still *more* love in

Harlequin Presents...